c

o

p

e

RULES OF APPROPRIATE CONDUCT

. . . . .

KIRSTEN ALENE

CONTENTS

For Cameron and Dad

ARTICHOKE

· · · · ·

STOLEN

All evidence points to the fact that documents were stolen.

#319 on row 7, aisle 2 shares thoughts in the break room at 3:00 PM on Saturday. #319 says: "An inside job."

No one is sure where the documents have been taken. No one is sure who the taker of the documents could be. No one ever leaves; they only go other places. No documents are ever gone; they are only somewhere different.

#'s 721 and 843 propose the formation of a Commission to The Office of Temporarily Misplaced Documents, block T, row 8, aisle 14. They propose a commission be dedicated to the investigation and retrieval of the stolen documents. #721 and #843 – Office of Organizational Issues, Office block D, row 3, aisle 2 – fear the worst.

PANIC

Four days after documents are stolen panic breaks out on H block. #'s 500-556 – Security 8, blocks H-J – are called in.

Arrests are made. When some, like #440 and #261, return to work, their supervisors will not be happy.

On A block, from where the documents were stolen, murmurs about the documents are as follows:

"...misplaced..."

"...bad system..."

"...worker's comp..."

"...high-risk block..."

TUESDAY

On Tuesday, #819 and I are walking around Garden block F. We are looking up at the perforated ceiling, when our shoulders touch for the briefest moment. The sound is like the soft, forgiving crunch of a cicada shell under a bare foot by a riverbank. #819 steps away, looking around scared of being seen. Garden block F is surveyed by The Office of Public Grounds Safety, S block.

We are glad the Office of Public Grounds Safety surveys us. We would not be caught on block D, where the Office of Public Grounds Safety turns a blind eye. #819 and I want to be surveyed. For now.

A little ways off, crouching in the daffodils on the border of F and K blocks, aisle 18, is a man in a lemon-colored jumpsuit. "Sniff" he smells one daffodil. "Check" he checks off one line on a notepad clutched tightly in his right fist. "Sniff," he smells one daffodil. "Check," he checks one line.

There is no number on his jumpsuit lapel. #819 hurries us in the other direction. His hand unintentionally approaches the indented spot at the base of my spine, right beneath the waistline of my jumpsuit.

INSPECTION COMMISSION

Office block A, row 4, aisle 7, becomes the home of the Commission for the Inspection of Suspicious Persons and Events Related to the Disappearance of Documents. #721 and #843 – Office of Organizational Issues, Office block D, row 3, aisle 2 – promptly approve the formation of this Commission, citing "Certain Fears" as cause for expediting the mandatory paperwork involved.

When they are alone at night and everyone else has gone home, #721 and #843 discuss missing documents over a game of backgammon. Some of the things that are said are these:

"We will not let documents be missing."

"There are many methods for controlling documents."

"Documents are never gone."

"We will reclaim these documents."

ARCHIVE BLOCK C.065

In Archive Block C.065, my cousin, #333, sits behind a long wooden counter and stamps rejected and de-circulated documents. He has been questioned by the Commission for the Inspection of Suspicious Persons and Events Related to the Disappearance of Documents about the missing documents. He calls me on the phone at 3:00 AM. He is breathing strongly, like someone who is very tired, into one end of the phone. I am breathing quiet like someone who does not want to wake someone (but who is also very tired) on the other end.

"Hello," he says, "It's #333. It's #333."

My cousin, #333, always repeats things twice to make sure that he is heard.

"Hey," I whisper, "It's me. It's 3 AM, why are you calling?"

"#602," he says, "#602."

"Yes, it's me, #333, what's wrong?"

My cousin is breathing very hard now. There is a little pause and I realize his voice is crying noises. I feel strange below my ribs. I feel strange.

"I'm coming over #333," I say, "I'm coming over right now."

9

"No…" #333 spits, almost before my mouth closes on the last word, "No…"

The phone clicks and there is no more sound. A body makes a little movement beside me. I almost reach a hand out to touch the soft, peach skin. Great wide, even tracts of it stretch from the crumpled sheets almost invisible in the darkness of Quarters – z block.

The next morning Archive Block C.065 is closed for public record examination procedures. #819 points to this sign and pretends not to have heard #333 call last night.

"Is that #333, your cousin?" he asks, still pointing at the sign on the clipboard outside the Archive Blocks. Some people stop and look at me.

"Yes," I say, "My cousin." But I am confused and do not say anymore. It is time to sit down.

I sit down.

#333

I do not want to leave Quarters – Z block. I am afraid of who is waiting outside my door now, to check where I am going. I am afraid now that I will not get Artichoke to Quarters – Z block, row 27, aisle 6, the residence of my cousin, #602. I am nervous that someone who is waiting outside of my door to check where I am going already knows that Artichoke is in my possession even though I told them last night that I had never seen any such thing.

I had never seen any such thing. Until I was handed Artichoke. A tall man said, "Take Artichoke to a place where no one will find it. Do not tell anyone where you take it."

Nothing is ever missing, it is always in another place. Quarters – Z block, row 27, aisle 6, Z.247.

ARTICHOKE

#333 was questioned about the missing documents in Quarters – block F, row 53, aisle 8, F.774 last night. This was a scheduled interview. The next day Archive Block C.065 was secured by the public record examination officials. In between Event A and Event B, #333 called me in Quarter block Z.247, where #819 slept quietly like a baby dolphin beside me.

Now #333 is sitting in my office on Q block, aisle 4, row 6. His arms and palms are dewy with little drops of perspiration.

"I've always looked up to you, 602. I've always looked up to you, 602. Since we were young. Young," #333 says.

This is a bad way to begin a conversation, where one person is sweating and the other is drinking iced tea in a tall glass.

"I have been your friend some time and I am going to ask you a thing," #333 says, "A thing. I am going to ask you a thing."

"Okay," I say, nodding, "Okay." I sip the tea and look at #333 over the foggy rim of the glass.

"I need you to do something for me." He takes a breath, his eyes are deep circles right up against my deep circles sitting in my wood-walled cubicle in Q block.

"I need you to do something for me."

"Anything," I say, leaning forward and taking #333's dewy, wet hand.

His red eyes dart to a document on my desk. He blinks rapidly and whispers, "Do not tell me what that is that you are working on. Working on."

"Okay," I say, confused.

"This something that I need you to do, this something that I need you to do," he says, so quietly that he is barely breathing as he speaks, "Is to put a thing in that document. To put a thing in any document. Do not tell me what it is or where it goes. Do not tell anyone." As he says this his hand uncurls my fingers and places a tiny piece of paper in the center of my palm. He curls my fingers back up, trembling. "You cannot know, no one can know, I cannot know. You cannot know."

This is the last thing that #333 says to me as he leaves my

wood-walled cubicle in Q block.

The tiny piece of paper says in plain, square handwriting: "Artichoke."

#819 MAKES HUMMUS

I am looking up at the ceiling when it is dark. I am thinking about the Artichoke. I cannot tell #819. I cannot tell anyone what happened to Artichoke. Nothing is ever gone. I don't know if anyone will ever find Artichoke. Last night I called #333 and moisture filled the room where #819 was making garlic hummus in the kitchen module of Quarters block Z.247. The rhythmic scraping of the metal fork on the metal bowl in the hand of #819 was like the sprinkler system in Food block C.

"#333" I whispered beneath the sprinkler sound, "#333, I did what you…"

There is a cacophonic static sound on the other end of the line, it is like an eruption of steam and I realize #333 is blowing air into the receiver. The room is very wet with the hotness of his breath. Everything in it is being blown on through the beige receiver. Perspiration falls from #819's milky forehead. A drop misses the metal bowl of hummus. The Quarters block is running with waterfalls of hot water.

"Nothing. You did what I nothing, #602," #333 whispers widely, "You did what I nothing."

I feel confused. I worry about Artichoke. I worry that someone will find the corner of it lifted a little. I wonder if someone will see it in Fax #600325 to Office block F.7.

I am trying not to tell #819 about Artichoke, but my silence is blocking up the room with water.

Finally, I have to speak. In the privacy of Quarters – Z block, I can wrap my small arms around the tall chest of #819. I can bury my face between his chicken-wing shoulder blades and dig my fingers all the way through his floral-patterned apron, into his soft and circular stomach.

#819, I force myself not to say, *My cousin, #333 came to me today.*

#819 wriggles around in the tight cocoon of my arms and stands with my not speaking open face between his hands that smell of garlic. They are the texture and size of cork-boards. His also open face is a planet. His small nose is curved upward. Through his nostrils I can see a forest of tiny bamboo stalks and pandas grazing with dedication.

The bowl of hummus is above my head. It is just above the water level. We are almost underwater now. The Quarters block always floods when somebody doesn't say a thing. It is a feature installed by the Ministry of Morality, Office block P, row 7, aisles 6-40. The Ministry of Morality occupies only one row. It permeates P block. #819 and I never visit P block.

The Ministry of Morality concerns many people. The Ministry of Morality concerns #819.

#409: FOOD BLOCK

I have felt a small tremor through the Mango Tree. It is growing tall now, up against the plaster of the ceiling. When I was here some time ago, the Mango Tree was in the palm of my hand. It was a yellowish, hairy splinter.

Large, official documents arrive on Monday.

In gold letters across the head of the page is written: "Inspection Commission." I have been summoned for examination by the Commission for the Inspection of Persons Potentially Related to the Current State of Affairs.

It appears that some documents have been stolen. But no one is suspicious of the height of the Mango Tree. Not yet, anyway.

I worry about Taller. I worry if Taller will be found between the bark and the soft, living tissue of its growing, sappy trunk.

I run a finger up expanding flesh. I can feel the pulse of a giant wooden heart, deep down inside the Mango Tree. And a tremor, like a shiver, in the wood.

THE FLOOD IS GETTING HIGHER,
WE ARE FLOATING

It would be alright to keep this secret of Artichoke from my #819 if the water level in Quarters block Z, Z.247 was not growing dangerously high. Up against the ceiling now, looking at one another over the bowl of hummus in #819's hands, #819 says: "You know I respect your privacy and everything, but I think you ought to tell me the thing you are not saying."

I agree and, treading water, I tell #819 what I have done with Artichoke and how it came to me. I tell #819 he can say nothing and he is thinking and we are silent as the water slowly recedes.

AWAKE

It is late. The water recedes steadily. #819 is sitting up in the kitchen. He is not making anything except a small clicking noise with his tongue and the little whisper, "Artichoke," every ten to fifteen minutes.

#602: MORNING

The flood recedes in the night. #819 is still worried in the kitchen and has not slept. There is nothing else to do. We leave Quarters block Z and walk down the dim-lit hallway of aisle 6. Arriving at Office block Q, row 5 aisle 19, Q.9021, I sit on the desk and look into the dark wood grain of the cubicle. Artichoke is the word I mouth. Artichoke is the word I make again, again, again, in the very dimmest quarters of my mind. Artichoke.

#819: OFFICE BLOCK Q,
ROW 14, AISLE 18, Q.9037

I am worried about #602. This morning I do not want to leave her in Office block Q.9021. She has the look of a mango tree in a thunderstorm. I want to put up a lightning rod close by, somewhere between row 5 and row 14. I think a lot about Artichoke.

Here are the things I do in Office block Q.9037:

1. Send fourteen faxes, all to the same number, 605-423-8437. I do not know this number. It is all the way in Office block X.77743. The nature of this block is unspecified.

2. Transcribe six files for Archive block C.065. This is the Archive block of #333, the cousin of #602.

3. Think about the little moony smile of #602.

4. Think about the often-soft reptile skin of #602.

5. Have visions of Artichoke being sent in a fax.

6. Receive an envelope with gold-embossed lettering from the Inspection Commission.

Then, at 4:07 PM I am looking straight up at the plaster ceiling. There is a splotch of ink high above me. It looks like it could be a hole. It looks like it could open up and reveal the twisting branches of a mango tree from Food block.

I cannot reach up that far.

That is all that happens at work. I type many things and I think about the octopus arms of #602.

BUTTERFLY

We notice the caterpillars beginning to appear on Tuesday. Yesterday, they were crawling a little from side to side.

"We should go to the doctor," I say.

"No," you say, "No, it will all be alright."

This isn't anything we haven't seen before. It isn't anything we can't learn to deal with.

You don't seem worried.

I know where this is all coming from.

It was the small typed word, "Butterfly" you cooked into the pasta that we made Sunday night.

Yes, I can say that it was surely in the pasta.

A DOCUMENT DOES NOT ARRIVE

A document has not arrived in Archive block C.7482. Confusion and suspicion erupt among the residents and workers surrounding block C.7482. No one can say where the document arrived. It arrived in some place. The place where it arrived is not the place where it was scheduled to arrive. The sender is interviewed by the Inspection Commission.

The sender is a man from Office block D. The sender is #017.

#017

Sometimes I am a large bird.

Sometimes I like to pretend that I can swoop down from the rafters of Garden block and kiss the heads of passersby.

The man in Office block D, row 10, aisle 14 visits my cubicle on Monday morning.

"#017."

"#475?"

"#017, I have a document for you to send."

"Alright."

"Here it is."

"Where do I send it?"

"Anywhere."

#475 turns to leave the cubicle. The document flutters to the desk.

"#475?"

"Yes?"

A pool of swelling, swirling water covers the brown shoes of #475.

"#475?"

I am alone in the cubicle in Office block D.

The document is short. It is fluttering, as if in a breeze from Garden block F. I reach for it with both hands.

A rustling can be heard from two delicate white wings which have grown from the back of the paper. I can feel it struggle for the air. I can feel it flutter in my icy fingers.

I cannot fax this document.

I cannot send this document.

I cannot let this document go.

INSPECTION COMMISSION

There is tension in Z block. No one is filing. No one is placing calls or faxes. No one is transcribing messages. No one is copying files. No one is adding up numbers.

The Inspection Commission, in brown bowlers that cover their eyes, moves through the block interviewing suspects.

#819 has stopped looking at the ceiling and is looking at the bowler hats of the Inspection Commission.

#017 IS ARRESTED PUBLICALLY

When the Inspection Commission moves into Office block D, #017 runs an errand to Accounting block R. When it is discovered that there is no real errand to be run to Accounting block R, #017 is retrieved by members of Security block T.01765.

#017's eyes are wet and so is his white collar. The low, loose jowls of his face quiver and shake. In aisle 17, #017 falls to his knees, the sound of bones hitting the tiles of the floor is like the sound of a mango tree being struck by lightening. There is a crackle in the air. It is the voice of #017. It is saying: "Never."

Large gray wings erupt from the back of #017's white shirt. They flap up and down and he rises up against the ceiling. He flaps joyously around block D. Everyone is watching but no one is speaking. Everyone in block D is watching.

#017 laughs. #017 swoops low over the heads of the people working in block D and twirls in the air.

A member of Security 8 throws a manual up into the air

and hits #017 squarely on the shoulder. #017 plummets to the ground and falls in a heap of gray feathers, scattering plaster and dust everywhere.

Water gushes from #017, gushes over workers and desks and chairs. People flee. Members of Security 8 run. People run faster. Desks and chairs, unable to run, are sinking under water.

#819: ANOTHER FLOOD

The floors and corridors begin to flood. #819 leaps up onto his desk and worries about the small, red shoes of #602 several rows away. His eyes are wide and confused and in them there is a word and the word is Artichoke.

EXPLOSION

An Explosion shakes Archive block C. Water rushes in through the walls. An ocean from the other side of Archive block C suddenly meets the flood of #017, still spreading. Alarms sound. Damp members of Security rush to the scene. Announcements are made.

#602 RUNS THROUGH WATER
TO ARCHIVE BLOCK C.065

#333

Water fills up the room. Water fills up the room.

Huge water mammals from Ocean block Q, aisles 3-10 swim past me. Huge water mammals swim past me.

I do not understand what is happening. Papers are everywhere. I do not understand what is happening.

I am floating up toward the ceiling. I am floating up.

TERRORISM

It has become apparent that terrorists have aligned themselves with those responsible for the stolen or missing documents. A wall was broken down in Ocean block Q. Manatees and Orca whales drift lazily past Archive block C. Flooded corridors are rife with tentacled squid and many species of salmon.

Action must be taken.

MANATEE

This is the first time we have seen Office block D. It is very nice. We may stay in Office block D. No telling.

#602

Get to Archive block C.065.
    Find #333.
    Get to Quarters block Z.247.
    Find #819.

#819 BEGINS TO FLOWER

The water leaking from the far away crumpled gray body of a suspect is leveling out at around six feet. Feathers drift past. As I stretch to reach the low wood wall of my cubicle and climb above the water level, the brown leg of my trousers lifts. Green and purple spines protrude through my sock.

I should not have taken the document containing Artichoke.

Other people are perched on the walls of their cubicles as Security 8 vacuums up the water.

Someone just received a fax. "A wall has broken down in Ocean block."

People mutter and glance.

Sure enough, a salmon flickers past around my purple ankle.

#333 CANNOT BE FOUND

I believe he must have gone home early. His green timecard is punched at 4:02 PM in the 'out' column.

Chills are running all down my spine and I am thinking of Artichoke with red red cheeks and cold toes. I have had to swim with manatees and whales all through Office block D. Now I cannot find my cousin.

#333 is not very old, but his eyes are sunken down into his face behind deliberate round glasses. He is not very loud and he is not very tall. Nothing about #333 is very anything. I cannot even tell what he looks like.

I am starting to think that maybe I do not know what he looks like.

Many people are perched up on tall file cabinets in Archive block C, just above the water level where no manatees or orca whales are swimming. "We have not seen #333 at all, no we have not seen #333 at all," they call back to me when I ask.

I wonder if Artichoke is in one of these cabinets but I know I cannot look.

#819 BAKES A PEACH AND TORTOISE PIE

It is a good thing Quarters block Z is so far from Ocean block. When I arrive home #602 is nowhere to be found. I can see her swallowed by a whale and my limbs begin to numb. This is a worse feeling than Artichoke weighing on me, than knowing a document was made missing.

Quarters block Z is covered in sea anemones. For a little while I just sit on the bed in Quarters block Z and stare up at the anemone ceiling. Opening and closing mouths smack at me, little spiny arms sign to me, minute tendrils oscillate in synchronicity with my exhalations.

If in fifteen minutes #602 is not back…

If in fifteen more minutes #602 is not back…

Fifteen more minutes…

To pass time I scrape anemones and starfish from the oven. I will bake a peach and tortoise pie.

#602: GARDEN BLOCK F

In the aisle across from this bench a man in a yellow jumpsuit smells a daffodil, "sniff," and makes a check mark on a notepad, "check."

"Sniff," shuffle shuffle, "check."

#333 is gone, is missing, cannot be found. Are people ever gone? Mightn't #333 have been swallowed by a whale? Transferred to another block? Made a sudden journey? Gone looking for me so that we are chasing each other around in circles, just missing each other's heels as we round corners?

"Sniff." Shuffle. "Check."

In my heart I can feel the untrueness of these things. I have looked everywhere a #333 could be found and have not found him.

I have reasons to believe that #333 was stolen.

I am crying.

"Sniff." Pause. Scowl. "Sniff." Scowl. Pluck. Crumple crumple. Scribble scribble. Shuffle shuffle.

PEOPLE ARE STOLEN

Under cover of many flowing black cloaks, people steal into the rooms of sleeping workers and take them. Black cloaked people hit and kick the workers. They put blacker bags on the heads of workers and draw them out into the aisles. There are no sounds.

#819 AND #602 FALL ASLEEP

The bodies of #602 and #819 are curved around each other like the rows of sweet corn in Food block.

21

MANGO TREE

#409 left some time ago. No one is here to run a soft, peachy finger along my heartbeating trunk. Stretching up I find the loneliness feels a lot like Taller.

MISSING

I am looking for my cousin, #333. He could not be found in places that he is usually found. He works in Archive block C, C.065. He is somewhat small, his hair is somewhat short, he has been known to wear spectacles. He is #333. If found, please contact #602: Quarters block Z, Z.247.

WANTED

Information regarding Missing Document code #305-D436 in connection with the word explosion, found buried in the wreckage of the recent wall-collapse in Ocean block Q. Reward.

IT IS NOW BELIEVED THAT THOSE RESPONSIBLE FOR THE DELIBERATE DESTRUCTION OF OCEAN BLOCK Q, AISLES 3-10, ARE CONNECTED TO THE

RECENT DISAPPEARANCE OF EVENT DOCU-MENTS CODE #305-D436 PGS. 7-9. THESE DOCU-MENTS WERE REPORTED STOLEN OR MISSING THURSDAY, 16/177

It is Wednesday. Several people have not reported to morning shift. It is still very early. Several people may have slept in. Several supervisors are not yet worried.

STOLEN

When my tired eyes wake up it is Wednesday. My body feels up against a cold part and I believe before my thick eyelids open that Quarters block Z must have flooded when #819 and I were lying in our dreams.

The cold part is not a flood.

The cold part is not water.

The cold part is the missing furnace body of #819.

MANY BODIES WAKE UP COLD

For the first time in months, several bodies in Quarters blocks F-Z wake up cold. No further explanation is offered by the Inspection Commission, who leave small gold tags on pillows which read: "Please report to Inspection Office, Office block A, Aisle 7, Row 4."

#602 is among those who wake in cold, empty beds.

The rows and aisles, still a little damp from the arrest of #7 and Explosion of Ocean block Q, feel hostile.

#819 SITS IN THE DARK AND THINKS OF OTHER WORDS

Artichoke.

Cherry.

Glasses.

Choir.

Studio.

Pea Soup.

Moonlight.

MISSING COUSIN

When I wake up without the warm love-tendrils of my #819

around me, I am seized instead by a little thrill of horror. I know that all of this leads back to Artichoke and I know that the only thing I must do is find my missing #819 and my missing cousin, #333.

A BLOCK

A strange feeling of aloneness gathers on my clothes as I dress. Everything is covered in it by the time I leave Quarters block Z for Showers block Z.

I only want to wash my face of all the loneliness but all of the sinks are taken and the dust is clouding my eyes and I am afraid to stand in the hall alone and wait.

I gather up some papers from the bedside table. One paper is a gold-embossed tag. I walk out of Quarters block Z.247.

It is time to visit A block and see if I can get back my #819 or make a trade or pay a fine or write a document.

I need to see #333, my cousin who is missing.

SECRETARY, A BLOCK, ROW 1, AISLE 4, A.0004

"8-1-9."

"I don't show that number registered in holding."

"I have this tag."

"I can schedule an appointment."

"I am looking for #8-1-9."

"I don't show that number registered in holding."

"I woke up to this tag."

"I can schedule you an appointment, it's no trouble."

"Do you know where I should go to locate #819."

"I'm sorry, I can schedule you…"

"Where should I go?"

Bee-hive haired secretary looks steadily at #602 for several seconds. "Continue on."

"Without him?" gasps #602, "You obviously haven't understood…."

"No." Beehive haired secretary gazes down Aisle 4 through the rest of A block. "Continue on."

"On to where?"

Bee-hive haired secretary removes horn-rimmed spectacles, uncurling coin-sized slip of paper that says: "Far."

"How far?"

"Far."

#602 stands up, Far between thumb and forefinger.

Bites pen and eyes near-sighted the little slip of paper tucked into the horn of her horn-rimmed glasses reading: "Far."

Stands up.

THE HEART IN #602

The heart beating in #602 is fast. It has been beating for the last twenty minutes, fast and loud When #602 thinks about the heart beating inside her, she is as scared as anyone has ever been to find a thing alive and with them that does not need her approval or consultation to act.

#602's eyes are wide open circles with darkish centers and red-ish frames. She has not slept. She has not eaten lunch in Cafeteria block Z or made toast in the mornings in their empty Quarters block Z.247.

#602's heart has been beating because a fax just came through twenty minutes ago. In the second line of the fifth page of the document was a word a bit askew. The word was Shoulder. The word was clipped and pasted. The word was Shoulder and #602 knows now that Artichoke is not the only word. That the words that are separated from their document are not just Artichoke but Shoulder, and maybe Standing, maybe Guile, maybe Pew, maybe Spaghetti.

New meaning comes to everything.

The heart in #602 cannot forgive the takers of her #819.

The heart in #602 cannot stop beating loudly, separately, brightly. Far. #819 is far. Perhaps another word is Far.

The heart itches badly.

#602

Other people's people are missing. They are sitting in A block, some are crying.

"I know where to go," I say, "We need to go far. We need to go soon. Our people have been taken."

The missing people's people continue to cry. Some stand and wipe their eyes.

#819

Am I in a prison? Am I underground? Am I alone?

WALKING VERY FAR

"We have been walking for a very long time," one person says.

"This is the farthest distance I have ever walked," says another person.

"I am tired of walking this very far distance," another says.

Another: "When will we stop this walking?"

Another: "Nothing is changing, no one is being found."

Another: "It is pointless to walk all this very far way – no one knows where the people that are missing have gone."

Another: "Mightn't they have just been reassigned?"

Another: "Of course they did not just disappear."

Another: "No one ever disappears."

Another: "But they do go other places."

Another: "Once there was a document that disappeared…" we have all forgotten that story and the person is interrupted by another.

Another: "Which places?"

Another: "We do not know these places, this is why we are walking."

Another: "It is a far way to walk."

Another: "We have been walking for a very long time."

#602: SCARED

Wherever we are headed, I already know it is not where #819 is. When I close my eyes and see him in the middle of an office, the office is hot, yellow, and covered in leaves like a garden. When I see my #819, his arched back, his hunched shoulder, his long, knobby toes like the knuckles of a mango tree, he is in this yellow, leafy room.

But in my dreams at night #819 is in a tall-walled grey stone chamber, not knowing me, and whispering through an open duct: "Artichoke."

THE SIGN FOR CABANA

"Cabana."

"What does it mean?"

"It means we must go farther."

It has golden edges and black text. It reads: "Cabana."

"Let's go," the manatee says.

ARTICHOKE

What is the purpose of a word if the word is not Artichoke. I have tired almost now of Artichoke, Elephant, Star and Olive. It is time to be rescued by #602. Or to escape this place tormented by a lack of #602. A lack of her long, tangled hair and seven moles.

It is believed that #333 is dead. The other words are hidden off. We are ready to be found by #602. We are ready to be found.

CEILING

There is nothing not under the ceiling. There is nothing not covered under plaster, styrofoam, wood.

After the sign for the Cabana, the covering is wood. Only some people are working. There are empty desks with empty chairs in empty rooms on every aisle. Stereos are playing old music and some people are dancing slowly.

We are full of quivering black organs and a little bit confused.

"I've never been here," #712 says.

"We've never seen a place like this," #684 says.

I am looking at the uneven floor. It is rocking like the waves in Ocean block. It is over another Ocean block. Or it is warped by too much silence.

I have never seen the Cabana. I have never been to this place. Or known this place. But I have never not known there were places farther. In the darkest pages of the fullest documents there was a whisper of farther. My cousin, #333, had known farther. #819 was known to say: "My 602, I do not know, but I hope of places farther."

I suddenly feel a great whale-missing of #819.

All things are very ugly.

"What is the Cabana?" I ask, turning to a wood-walled cubicle occupied by a hunched-over body.

"What is the Cabana? I must know-" There is no response. I turn the body around. Electrical sockets are in its eyes. They spark benignly.

"On." I step back. "Further on."

IT'S GOING TO BE REALLY
INCONVENIENT WHEN YOUR EYEBROWS TURN
INTO BUTTERFLIES

First of all, we don't have any way of knowing when they will emerge from their chrysalis. It could be in three hours. It could be in fourteen days. It could be in a year and a half. It could happen at a bad time. Like when you are in a meeting with your supervisor. Like when we are making love. Like when we are walking around in Ocean block.

If your supervisor sees two yellow butterflies erupt from the center of your face he may think that you are insulting him. You may be transferred to another block. You may be transferred to Security. You may be put in prison.

If two small yellow wings unfold from over each of your eyes while we are making love and I am kissing your forehead, my chin may be tickled and I may cry out in surprise. Others in the block way wonder what the noise is.

If we are underwater when your eyebrows become two butterflies, they may get wet and drown. They may lose the perfect powder dusting on their frail wing skeletons. They may ingest the ocean water and evolve into great ocean predators. They may disrupt the ecosystem.

BLUISH TARPAULIN

We sleep in a deserted corridor. These rows and aisles are un-numbered. These walkers seem scared. They seem tired. They seem bluish to me, when I open my eyes lying horizontal on the floor. Waiting for a sleep to come. Maybe Sleep is a word. I grow sure that Artichoke is not the reason. Many people are gone. There have been missing secretaries and missing interns and missing copyists in every quadrant, increasing in number as we pass through every successive block growing (suppos-edly) closer to the Cabana.

The bluish forms of many sleeping walkers have curled up against one another because their bodies are cold on the flat stone floor. They are rising gently and falling in relative unison.

I squint my eyes close together.

Now these walkers look like a crumpled, bluish tarpaulin.

PROJECTS IN THE MIND OF #819

In the backest little project of my mind, I am suspicious that Artichoke came from the missing documents.

In real life, I am blooming dangerously and my heart is growing softer and softer and resonating less and less with the sound of a number I remember like very quiet music.

DOOR

Around midday we discover a large door in the corridor. Along the edge of the door words are gouged into the wall which extends to the ceiling and over every aisle as far as we can see. This door is the only door we can see although smaller doors may be located along the wall. Along the edge of the door the words gouged into the wall read: MEA CULPA, PECULUM, MEA CULPA.

#209

"This is obviously a trap." This is what #209 says.

"We must go further." This is what #602 says.

"There may be terrors lurking behind this door." This is what #087 says.

"We may be in terrible danger." This is what #340 says.

"Our missing numbers may be behind this door." This is what #065 says.

"There's only one way to find out." This is what the manatee that joined us says.

GOATS IN THE MACHINE

There is a vast cavern. Goats are moving like ants in lines, balancing large stacks of documents on their horns, on their backs, tied to the bottoms of their feet like leaf cuttings. The vast cavern that goats fill is cut by enormous columns. The columns grow like trees up into the ceiling of the cavern. But they are not trees, which are homes to birds and bearers of fruit. They are home to goats and bearers of documents which rise and fall from them in large baskets suspended by intricate pulley systems. Documents are flying upward, they are plummeting downward, they are being faxed and copied with remarkable speed and precision.

The ceiling in the cavern is so high that, at first, the manatee can be heard crying out behind: "But the ceiling! Where is the ceiling?" Many of the walkers gasp and shriek.

Each of the goats emits a sputtering flame from one horn. The ceiling in the cavern is dimly lit by the sputtering of the goats. A large goat passes by the open door. It bleats in the face of #209, who screams loudly, drawing the attention of other goats. As it turns away, the flame of its horn winks out of existence, replaced by a curling wisp of smoke. It stops mid-stride. Another goat lays down its stack of documents and approaches the now-shadowy goat. The goat reaches into the pocket of its silk vest and draws out a tiny black stone. The goat strikes the stone with its cloven hoof and sparks shower the head of the shadowy goat, who bleats once, then continues on, its candle re-lit. It is clear to the walkers that goats are powered by fire.

After this magnificent performance, #209 is intrigued. The walkers walk into the hall.

THE NOBLE BADGER

"Our love is greater than the love of the loneliest creatures. Greater than the most far-apart sea mammals, greater than the highest ceiling ever known, greater than the love of the most elusive creature in Park block D: The noble badger.

"The love of #602, no, the love of #602 cannot quail or ebb. It cannot shake or quiver or wane. Though I may become an artichoke, the most delicious of flowering vegetables, though I may transform, regress to my most elemental, vegetative state, the love of #602 cannot, will not, wane.

"Find me. Find me #602."

This is what I hear late into the nights as I am lying in my cot, trying to coax sleep into me from outside the window. It is a nice monologue to sleep on. I see that I am becoming Moonlight and I think that, in similar fashion, this lover of #602, is becoming Artichoke. I, myself, never liked artichokes. Perhaps I might now, now that I am Moonlight. Much has changed since the paling of my face, since the shimmering of my fingers began.

A PRESENTATION IN DETAINMENT FACILITY, INSPECTION BLOCK G.057

The document has been disbursed. In retrospect, the authorities see the cleverness of the plan. What the disbursers could not have foreseen was the bizarre and dangerous power of the document. The power, indeed, of all documents to persist, despite any attempts to destroy them. The most disturbing news to reach A block, of course, is the news of those that received the articles of the stolen documents.

Some, the receivers of benign words such as 'The' and 'A' saw little manifested effect. One cooperative suspect, #447, reported that her gender had suddenly and unexpectedly changed after the receipt and attempted digestion of the word "He."

DREAM

#819 is running toward me. He is running up the trunk of a mango tree with the word Taller. He is coming closer. He is running and sweating and gasping. He stumbles. He trips. He calls out. Up the long, rough trunk of the mango tree, he calls out to me: "#602!" He calls: "#602!"

The mango tree is growing faster than he is running. It

is rocketing upward with the speed of Taller. It is burrowing into the plaster ceiling. #819 is running, dodging chunks of plaster and waterfalls of dust particles. The mango tree has broken into the plaster. There is only more plaster above the plaster. And more. And more. The mango tree is wending its way through channels of endless plaster, powdering the white cement. I am calling down to #819.

Please.

Please wake up.

I wake up.

LETTER FAXED FROM OUTER BLOCK XXX D.64

Dear #743,

We are very far out now. Someone is beginning to turn into an Asian pear. Their soft, green skin becomes smoother and shinier every day. Still no news of the missing people. There has been no sign that anyone we know has been here but everyone we meet says to continue on. There is indication of a place called "Cabana." Now, our hopes are in the Cabana.

Will write again soon.

Much love,

#660

INTERROGATION FILE, SUSPECT #819

"What is your connection to the document code #305-D436?"

"Document what?"

"Code #305-D436."

"My department deals with code 100 level documents. I've never even seen a 300 level document."

"Is that the truth?"

"Of course it is – I work in Office Q block."

"What were your intentions when you took the pages 7-9 of document code #305-D436 out of circulation?"

"I'm not sure what you're talking about. My department handles code 100 level documents. I work in Office block Q. I work with #602."

"Where did you initially hide pages 7-9 of document code #305-D436 after you located and took them out of circulation."

"I feel as if you are assuming a lot."

"Your feelings are not relevant to this conversation."

"Are you going to tell me what's happening to my arms?"

"We're... really not sure."

"Are you going to do anything about it?"

"That depends."

"On what?"

"Your cooperation."

"I'm cooperating."

"Then tell us how you came in contact with pages 7-9 of document code #305-D436."

"I told you, I don't know what you're talking about."

"Ahem."

"All I know is that #602's cousin was upset about a thing, and that thing was this tiny slip of paper that she had. I read it and I took it. Now I am here. Now #602 is somewhere. I am turning green and leafy. And no one is doing anything. We are all just sitting."

"Until you are willing to reveal how, why, and when you took the documents from circulation, nothing can be done."

"But I..."

"Nothing. Nothing can be done."

"I..."

"Nothing."

MUCH RUMMAGING RESULTS ONLY IN CONFUSION

When we push open the next enormous wooden door, we are faced with low-walled stone cubicles. Some are holding goats.

Some are holding people. Most are holding documents. These documents are yellowing and messy. There are no fax machines, typewriters, or telephones sitting on the desks of these cubicles. There are splotches of ink on every surface.

"What is this?" asks #823.

His skin is the color and texture of an Asian Pear. His midsection is becoming bloated and round.

But he is not yet ripe.

Some goats walk past us. One bleats curiously at #823.

I walk ahead of the other walkers, down an aisle with antique numbers crookedly hung on long wrought iron hangers, protruding from stone cubicle walls. There are particles of straw and dust in the air. Windows are high on the walls. The floor is covered in a fine layer of sand and ground up straw.

In one cubicle, a man is standing taking single pages of a stack of documents as tall as his cubicle, folding them in half carefully, and placing them in a smaller stack.

"Excuse me?" I ask.

"Yes?" says the man, looking up at me through glasses that make his eyes enormous.

"I was wondering if you had seen anyone around here, anyone that looked lost, anyone that looked like they were becoming an artichoke."

"Let me see," the man says, tapping the side of his face with one finger. His fingers are dirty and curled up like tired snakes. "Now let me just see."

"It's just, we've been walking for a long time and, well, we were told that we should find the Cabana."

The man's eyes snap up. "Yes," he says quietly, "Let me just see."

"So, we should?" I ask, "We should find the Cabana."

The man edges past me carefully and walks out into the aisle. He pauses for a moment, looks both ways then hurries away from the walkers. Several rows away, he stops and glances over his shoulder toward me. "Aren't you coming?"

"Oh," I say, "Yes."

I look back toward the walkers nervously. No one is watching me. Everyone is looking around, talking quietly to one another. #823 is crying silently to one side of the group as a goat stares at him hungrily.

The manatee is scratching its head.

I follow the giant-eyed man.

We walk for some time. We walk down some stairs in one cubicle. We walk up some stairs in another.

The giant-eyed man says nothing.

I say nothing.

There is nothing to say.

When we stop we are in a cubicle made of documents. There are documents up to the almost-out-of-sight ceiling. There are documents on the floor. There are chairs made of documents. The desk is many documents. Some of them are worn and yellowing. Some are new. The giant-eyed man crawls under the desk.

He dismantles the left front leg of one chair.

He climbs partway up the wall.

"Let me see now," he says, "Let me just see now."

"Thank you for all of the trouble you're taking," I say, my heart beating. I can feel #819. I can feel his heart beating in mine. I can feel the heart of the giant-eyed man, beating fast as he scurries up and down the document wall whispering, "Let me just see now."

After an immeasurable amount of time I can feel the little indentations that my feet have made in the documents below me. I want to sit down, but I don't want to move in case my movement disturbs the rummaging of the giant-eyed man.

At last he calls from beneath an almost dismantled chair: "Ahah!"

"I believe this is the man you are looking for," the man says, backing out on his knees from under the chair, a crumpled sheet of paper in his fist.

I snatch it from his outstretched hand and read.

LETTER

Fax #3290128200029394
ATTN: #22345
Archive block XVVXI G.09873
From: #20892Cabana

Seen being led into Inspection block D, 16/1017, time: 7:04 am, one pale green man.

Suspect related to the recent disappearance of pages 7-9 of document code #305-D436.

Please note: man is the color of fresh asparagus.

Action required.

File under: Document incident code #6674-H6.

Hope all is well.

Sincerely,
#20892
Cabana

The second page is a small ink drawing. It is of a man being led into an open door. The man looks sad.

My heart plunges into the bottom of my body. I feel it twitching feebly inside me. Our suspicions are confirmed. The giant-eyed man is staring at me, his huge glasses askew.

"Thank you," I say, clutching the document to my chest.

"It's a duplicate," he says.

"Thank you."

I run back down the aisles as fast as I can. I can only see goats everywhere I look. I need to find the walkers.

Our suspicions have been confirmed. The Cabana is where we must go.

I am almost back to where I left the walkers. They are still huddled together. They have not gone on.

I wave the document in the air above my head.

No one is looking.

I remember I should have asked the giant-eyed man where to go to find the Cabana.

There are only goats around.

AROUND NOON

Around noon, the wooden floors become stone beneath our feet, and then, quickly, dirt.

People become more scarce.

Some goats walk back and forth across the rows and aisles we wander through. They bleat angrily at us, as if we are interrupting their work.

#823 flinches when they bleat.

The ceilings descend on us again. They are dark. Heavy wooden rafters stretch low across the aisles.

#823 watches warily as a goat on a crossbeam glares down at him. "Shoo," he whispers, his voice cracking.

"Let's just go on," says #660.

The goat bleats louder. Another goat stops in its tracks and eyes #823, who has stopped walking beneath the two goats.

A third goat peers out of a small stone cubicle. "Bgahhhh," it says, glancing at the other goats above us.

"Ahhh!" says #823.

The goat walks out of the stone cubicle and takes a swift bite out of the soft green pear flesh of #823.

"Ahhh!" says #823, louder.

Another goat appears behind the manatee who, surprised, steps out of its way.

The other goat takes a chomp out of the knee of #823. #823 drops to the ground. The goats on the rafters descend via the tops of the stone cubicle walls.

"Run," #823 whispers, his wide pear eyes bloodshot and bulging as the goats tear into his pear flesh, "Run."

We run.

What else can we do?

The manatee is crying.

DELEAFING

When I awake, there are black suited men in the cell. My window has been blocked up with a pink pillow.

"#819," says one of the black suited men. His eyes are dark circles in the pink light shining around the edges of the pillow. "#819, your lack of cooperation leaves us with no choice. You must reveal how you acquired pages 7-9 of document code #305-D436 or face imminent deleafing. If you reveal the whereabouts of the words 'sand,' 'microbial,' or 'parallel,' we will postpone the deleafing."

"What does that even mean, 'sand?'… 'microbial?' I don't know what those things mean, I don't know where they are. I don't want to be deleafed! Please!"

"You leave us with no choice, #819," says a different black suited man.

"Begin," says another.

Two black suited men step forward. They grab onto either side of a wide, fleshy leaf near the bottom. I feel a gentle tugging, then a jerk. Pain. My body is a fire of pain. I cry out. The men pull harder, bracing themselves with their feet on my middle. The leaf comes free.

Blood gushes forth.

They grab hold of one another.

MANGO TREE: CONTEMPLATIONS

Screams echo through block F. Since the departure of #409, I think a lot about the word outside Garden block F. I think about the sounds. I think about the voices trembling in the plaster. I think a lot about the plaster grating against my bark. I think a lot about the powdery white material leeching precious moisture from my fruits but I continue growing taller.

There is nothing strong enough to stop me now.

The scream that is echoing through block F is the scream of a vegetable. I can tell. All of the mangos on my limbs and lying mushy on the ground around me are crying out as well. They are crying back but no one can hear them – not since #409 departed.

I am tired of being in this garden block. I am tired of hearing screams like this vegetable scream which chills the veins of my wide leaves and puts more evil in the plaster.

Something must be done.

So I grow Taller. I will grow into every block, into every cubicle in every block, into every aisle and row. Plaster will carry me there. And Taller.

ARTICHOKE HEART

Blood is around me. I wonder if I am just a heart now, transformed by the word from #602, that evil word, that evil document of evil words.

What was she doing with such a thing? She should have known better than to accept a suspicious thing like that.

I do not care about #602 now. Not after my full flowering green and purple body has been deleafed and defiled.

#602 did not even look for me or wonder where I was. #602.

She will not love me anyway, as just a purple heart.

THE RECOVERY OF DOCUMENT CODE #305-D436

Since the explosion of Ocean block, inspectors have been combing walls and desk chairs for words. Wine was found when a telephone began to leak. Summer was found when a wall began to bud and flower. Other pieces of document code #305-D436 were discovered in such places as a wardrobe, a pencil, a park bench, a mango tree. Extractions have begun. It may be years before all of document code #305-D436 is recovered.

THE RECOVERY OF TALLER

I can feel my limbs drawing out of every tunnel. I can feel my branches recede. In time I will be a single fruit. In time not even #409 will recognize my bark. Years pass.

WALKING

No one is quite sure how long we have been walking. We cross lakes and rivers now from time to time and forests of abandoned documents tended by single workers, by single goats. A tree grows in the aisle ahead of us, documents have fallen all around it. Some are decayed, some are grown through, some are illegible.

Here the ceiling is very low. We must crouch to crawl beneath it. Soon it will be high again, soon we will see more workers with electric faces or goats with candlehorns.

WINDOW IN THE LIGHT

"Come with me," the moonlight in the window says.

"What?"

"Come with me, there was a mango tree in the next cell but it has withdrawn. I have heard you talk every night."

"Come with you? But how? I cannot get out of this cell."

"You are much smaller now and bars like these cannot hold just a heart."

"Alright."

"Come quickly. I am getting others. There are many."

"Here I come."

MANGO TREE

Some people cannot move on their own now. A brown horse
had three legs sawed off long ago. A beautiful antique mirror
was broken. We carry one another through the passages the
Mango Tree made with Taller. Now some of us want to be
people again. They are thinking of going back, to be changed
like the Mango Tree was long ago. They have forgotten what
the cells were like, they have forgotten what we did. At night,
we sit and talk about the tunnels, about the little animals, the
spots of bright sunlight that show through every so often, and
about document code #305-D436. From what we can gather
it was a document about a happy time. From what we can
gather there was a lot of fruit, music, joy, and love.

Here in the plaster tunnels the Mango Tree carved we
gather fruit from the tiny mango trees it left behind. We dig in
the plaster until water leaks through and we drink the chalky
liquid, our face ghost-like, smiling.

I remember that I must have loved a person in that time
when I was becoming. I cannot remember her name. I remember a number, that number is 602.

NO MAKING

Today we cross a vast flooded block. There is no end in sight,
only the gentle edging sound of waves lapping at the grey
wooden walls. The farther out we go the older everything becomes. This wood is bare, unfinished, rough.

The manatee says to itself, "Ocean."

It must be homesick.

Our boat is made of straw that has fallen from the ceiling.
Our oars are the spines of whales. We are heading out. We are
heading toward the Cabana.

DOLPHIN SON

· · · · ·

When we first moved here, we always felt lucky when it rained. It was a special treat to see our city in various states of panic and unrest – during protests in the courthouse square, in snow-storms, shopping holidays downtown, or in the rain. Pride and wonder swelled in us when bridges rose inconveniently in our path to let tall ships slide by underneath them, when train bells sounded, halting us on our bikes to stand in the cold for a quarter hour while box cars rattled past.

At the beginning, we still felt that sort of wonder. The wonder of witnessing a fatal car accident, a derailed train, a downed power line, a flooded sidewalk. It still felt like magic when the rain started. Now that it's been two years, and the rain has never stopped, it feels more like magic when for an hour or so the downpour transforms into a drizzle, and the world is quiet and calm.

These times come with rapidly decreasing frequency now. River levees break upstream, hills and embankments collapse every day, sending waves of water down already water-worn canals to the river below us. Most houses are two feet under-water down here in the valley. No matter how much sand we put down, the water keeps rising.

Even the old houses in the hills are building themselves up on stilts and platforms. It feels dream-like to see these Victorian gingerbread mansions rise up swaying on huge cement pillars among the treetops. There are some with magnificent porches, whole yards with artificially crafted hillocks and greenhouses and undercover patios with grills and fire pits. There are some pathways between them and little landing pads for private helicopters.

When my husband was working, we would all go up there together to deliver the mail, slogging through impassible, unused mud roads with huge chunks of asphalt jutting up from where pieces of it had sunk into the soft, lazy ground.

Now no one thinks about the mail anymore, and my husband mostly stays at home, building our raft. We are preparing for our departure.

***

We've been experiencing a shortage of fresh vegetables and fruit. The only food left was canned and packaged months ago. Some residual apples – previously frozen in warehouses in Yakima for a year – have been deposited in soggy cardboard boxes outside the grocery store.

We trudge across the Burnside Canal in a closely huddled pack of people dressed in rain boots and snow pants. Most of the pavement has been pried up by the continuous surge of brown water and our feet slip over wet, round river stones and bits of trash washed down from the hills. Caleb, my son, slips into a hole and disappears beneath the surface. I see him flap around delightedly in the rushing water before I reel him up by the seat of his pants, using the tether with which all children nowadays are anchored to their parents. He was once a child with an impossibly strong aversion to water. Bathing him had been a nightmare. But since having spent what is now the majority of his life in the rain, he has begun to take to the water like a fish.

***

When we arrive home with the apples, my husband is bailing out the bathroom.

"Tell Dad we're home," I say, lifting Caleb out of the downpour, over the sandbag barricade, and onto the carpet.

Caleb plops down onto his knees and tugs at his rain boots. They are glued onto his legs and several sizes too small.

Dad peers out of the bathroom through muddy safety goggles. "We've sprung a leak in the bathroom."

"I can see that," I say, jumping over the sandbags to join Caleb on the floor. We pry each other's feet out of our boots and Caleb backs out of his too-large raincoat like a cat. His red long johns are patchy and worn. He shakes his head and runs a full circle around the room before jumping onto the couch in front of the radiator. He wriggles his bare toes a few inches away from the hot metal.

"They are saying at the store that they're cutting all of the funding at the dams this week," I say over the rhythmic dunk and splashing sound of bailing. I step over the sandbags in the bathroom doorjamb, wading into the small lake that was our bathroom earlier in the day. "They're probably evacuating everyone." Splash. Splash. My husband's t-shirt is plastered to his chest and arms with brown water and sweat. His arms bulge and strain with each bucket. The muscles twitch in his neck.

"Are we going to be ready?" I ask.

He removes his plastic goggles, grabs his head with one hand, like he's steadying himself for a big jump or a balancing act.

"It's impossible," he says hoarsely. Caleb is singing 'Row Row Row Your Boat' in the living room. "We won't be ready for weeks, We've got so much taken out on credit at the store already, and look at this," he gestures to the bathroom floor, then the roof, from where a steady stream of water splashes down into a big red bucket.

I put a hand on his shoulder. "We don't need a roof where we're going."

"But we need one to get there," he says.

***

If the levee breaks from pressure or if another whale breeches on the sea wall, a tidal wave of water is going to wash away our little two room house, and all the other houses on this street, all the houses in the city. While canned broccoli cooks on the stove, I finish up the big white sail I've been patching together from old socks and bed sheets. It's gotten quite large. I only hope the mast is strong enough to hold it.

Caleb's skin looks pale and grey. No amount of vitamin D supplements will give a child's skin the pink glimmer of natural sunlight. His father is worried. His father shoves his own small stack of broccoli onto Caleb's plastic dinner plate. "Eat that, kid." Caleb makes a face like a goldfish.

His father worries, but Caleb will be fine. I've seen him splash around in the Burnside Canal, I've watched him under the water at Lake Chapman. He's already evolving. He's already becoming the thing that's meant to live in this new city.

After dinner I pull the snow pants onto Caleb and grab a screwdriver and an axe from the flooded bathroom. "If we can't get the things we need on credit, we'll make them ourselves," I tell Dad. Caleb squeals like a car braking hard on a wet road.

"All right," Dad says, opening the hall closet to a cascade of old gardening tools and a rusty blue wheelbarrow, which he wrenches free of a nest of old tomato cages and fishing poles. The paint is chipped off in a dapple pattern; the surface is rocky with rust-boils.

46

Caleb clambers into the wheelbarrow and we lift him up and over the sandbags, down the rickety wooden staircase, sliding on the fine layer of moss and algae growing on the surface of the wood. The yard is a mudbath.

For a second or two, Caleb's father and I remember our yard, how it used to be in the beginning. It was a gold and green oasis, a life-explosion of succulent fruits and heavy-scented flowers. If we were rich, I think, we would bring this mud patch with us, up into the air like the Victorian houses in Nob Hill.

The tire of the wheelbarrow sinks into the thick muck as I run back up the staircase to lock the door. Our little raft is close to finished. There is only the left side of the house hanging pathetically over a partially completed wooden box enclosing four big, flat, empty water tanks of various sizes. A fifth tank juts up from the mud below. A peach fuzz layer of moss covers everything. The rain patters consistently around us, making the mud-yard shiver and shine with water ripples. I feel a moment of tremendous peace and calm coming before I notice that Caleb is in the mud, splashing around and wriggling with delight. His father lifts him back into the wheelbarrow and looks at me curiously. "Come on, Dad," I say, pulling on his garbage bag sleeve.

The trees are soft and pulpy, waterlogged and just beginning to rot from the inside out. In an hour we have gathered enough to finish the raft. On the way back home, we see signs with letters all run together in plastic sleeves posted over light posts and construction signs. There are all these meetings going on in people's houses, in office buildings, all over the city. The meetings are about what we will do when the dams break. As we stack the logs up on the wheelbarrow, we wonder which of these meetings we should be attending.

Caleb is underwater again, in a small pond, slipping in and out of sight, swimming. I tell my husband that we should attend none of these meetings. We will be fine.

The dusky grayness of daytime is fading, the rains sound quieting as they do each night, and Caleb, soaked through his raincoat and his snow pants, sleeps on the topmost log, clinging to the surface with his shiny gray arms.

There is hammering late into the night, the sound of logs splitting, the ting of aluminum siding, the thunder sound of plastic wedges boring into soggy planks. Our neighbors in their nightgowns come to their windows to scowl and tut through the curtains, not brave enough to come out and scold us in person. And as the sun rises we slide into the house and crawl under the covers of our big, frameless bed and hold our sleeping son. He has never been as sound or peaceful a sleeper as now, now that he is growing.

His eyes are large and round beneath puffy, bruise-colored eyelids like lanterns shut off for the night.

We fall asleep at once, the moorings all untied, our house balanced on its makeshift stilts, ready to be set adrift with the rest of our neighbors and be carried out to sea, down the coast, across the Pacific, to a watery paradise where nothing but sea spray falls from the sky and our dolphin son can frolic in the rainbow-capped waves, soaking in the hot bright sun that warms the water to a balmy bath temperature.

In our sleep we feel a lurching, a gentle swaying, and we're off.

EARL

We've done just fine since the stegosauruses came. In the be-ginning it was difficult, being the only food source. A lot of us were eaten, too many to count, too many to really remember. I like to think the carnivorous dinosaurs enjoyed us. Although, as with all reptiles, it is hard to read their facial expressions.

When the government finally declared itself uninvolved and withdrew its forces, we took up residence in an overgrown grove of peach trees. The sweet smell of rotting fruit, we think, is what masks our meaty scent, hiding us like a thick cloud of smoke.

We spend a lot of days making and remaking tents out of blankets and sheets that we hang between the low branches of the peach trees. Sometimes we lie on the ground and watch in-sects crawl across the layers of rotting fruit and foliage, make-believing we are small enough to ride on their backs across the brown-orange mountain-scape or light enough to cling to their little double-pronged feet as they take off into the air.

Originally we built houses, but the artificial amalgama-tion of walls and doors and all the wasted space became sad to us. So, we took them down and live stretched out under our blanket-tents, covered in mottled sunlight.

Occasionally one of us gets eaten, but they always return, smaller and more compact, with shorter limbs and huge, staring bright eyes. When they come back, they smell like rotting peaches, sickly sweet and browned all over.

But sometimes we go months without a carnivorous dinosaur sighting. During these times, some people say, "The dinosaurs are gone," and some other people say, "We imagined all of that." Some of those people are people who have been eaten. Only one person has been eaten twice.

We write long letters to everyone on the outside and deliver them by carrier pigeon. The man who has been eaten twice is named Earl. He has a coop of brown and white pigeons that carry letters to people on the outside. The long leaves and branches of the peach trees have grown out and over the pigeon cage by Earl's yellow tent. He has one window in his tent that is an uneven rectangle. Every time we see it we want to straighten it, but the window is cut from fabric. He hands us pigeons through the window like little fluttering loaves of bread, with both hands wrapped around them so carefully you would think he wasn't holding them at all. Maybe this is why pigeons only come back to Earl—even if you want them to come back to you. Earl's pigeons are named Sirius, all of them, after the brightest star.

Earl fed dinosaur meat to some of the pigeons, and after several years, those pigeons grew huge and scaly. The huge dinosaur-eating pigeons are named Calyphus and they are for long distance deliveries.

We are a long distance from all of the people who receive our letters, but the Sirius pigeons can handle that long distance. The Calyphuses are only used for long distances such as overseas and to the North Pole.

Some of us have family at the North Pole. One of us wants to leave and join them. His name is Earl. But he is not the Earl who has been eaten twice. All of us are named Earl. But one of us has been eaten twice and one of us wants to move to the North Pole.

Earl is sick to death of peaches. We know because he says this a lot. What you say a lot is important here, especially when it is dark and the only light comes from words hitting the trunks of the peach trees. No one knows why words hitting the trunks of the peach trees makes the only light we can see by, but it is how we see at night.

The light attracts the stegosauruses who like to graze on the moldy peaches around us. The stegosauruses will eat around a stretched out body on the ground, making a perfect human body shape of moldy peaches. Their huge black tongues sometimes flick out over the skin of the body that is stretched out on the ground, making sure it is not a delicious rotting peach. The black tongues tickle, but they are exfoliating and good for the skin.

Earl, who is sick to death of peaches, does not want stegosauruses to be in the peach grove eating moldy peaches and licking bodies, even though their black tongues are exfoliating. He says he is sick to death of stegosauruses. But the stegosauruses don't mind if Earl is sick to death of them. Earl has applied for a visa and wants to move to the North Pole. Every time a Calyphus arrives, Earl, who is sick to death of stegosauruses and peaches, runs toward the pigeon coop and jumps up and down. He looks very silly, as if he is being burned by the ground through the soles of his shoes until Earl, who has been eaten twice, comes out and hands him the letter the Calyphus has brought.

No one but Earl, who has been eaten twice, is allowed to touch the Calyphuses since one Calyphus ate a person. When the person came back we changed his name to David because he had not been eaten by a dinosaur, but by a pigeon. This seemed to be a very important distinction.

David is not afraid of the Calyphus that ate him. David has said a lot that to fear a thing that eats you is as silly as to fear a thing that didn't eat you. "I do not fear a peach," David says, "I do not fear that Calyphus."

The Calyphus that ate David has expressed a lot of interest in eating David again. Earl, who has been eaten twice, says the Calyphus has developed a taste for human flesh. Some people think we should kill that Calyphus, but whenever anyone says so, Earl, who has been eaten twice, begins to cry. David says it is wrong to kill a pigeon when you can let a pigeon live, that he will never stand for the killing of the Calyphus that ate him. Sometimes Earl lets the Calyphus chew on his arm. Sometimes someone else feels like letting a Calyphus chew their arm, so they let the Calyphus that ate David do it. No one else has been eaten by that Calyphus.

Today a Calyphus swoops low over our heads as we watch insects crawl over the rotting peaches. It makes a cooing pigeon sound. Earl, who is sick to death of peaches, calls from his tent: "Is that a Calyphus?" We all laugh as Earl runs over the rotting peaches and through the tree trunks.

We usually don't make any noise in the daylight because there are a lot of carnivorous dinosaurs out in the daylight. But no one tells Earl to stop making noise because it is funny to watch him hopping up and down, waiting for a letter from the North Pole.

No one believes Earl will ever be allowed to travel to the North Pole to meet his family.

David is not watching Earl. Instead of laughing at Earl, David is making a trench in the rotting peaches with his middle finger. A beetle approaches the trench, and David watches it closely. The rest of us are still laughing at Earl, but David is watching the beetle.

None of us understand why anyone would want to leave the peach grove. Earl, who is sick to death of peaches, says his family is waiting for him. He has a photo of his mother. She looks old and strict. We do not understand why someone would want to go to the North Pole to be with an old, strict mother.

David says that Earl, who is sick to death of peaches, has a sad heart. Earl is too aggravated by peaches and stegosauruses

52

and a lack of communication from the North Pole to tell us he has a sad heart.

David is still not watching the Calyphus or Earl. He is watching the beetle. We tried to name the insects in the peach grove, but we'd forgotten all the names besides Earl, Sirius, Calyphus, and David. The beetle falls into the trench that David made with his middle finger. It is on its back, kicking its tiny two-pronged legs. David lowers his finger and the beetle's legs flail as they curl around the finger like a life preserver. David lifts the beetle from the trench and places it in his beard.

Whenever a baby is born, everyone grows a beard to celebrate—even the women. The only things that do not grow beards are the baby, who will grow one later, and the stegosauruses that sometimes come into the peach grove to eat the rotting peaches on the ground. Stegosauruses do not grow beards.

Today I received a letter from my sister. She lives with a nomadic tribe of hunters in Africa. The tribe hunts tigers, and my sister is studying them to write a book about nomadic tribes who hunt tigers in Africa. She sends her love to David and me, and says to kiss the new baby twice if we get the chance.

She says the tigers are upset about being hunted and that this should make a really nice chapter in her book, which is already pre-selling copies across the country.

My sister's name is EARL. She writes with all capital letters. She writes her name at the bottom of her letters like this:

EARL

She asks if anyone has been eaten lately. I will write her back to say the last person to be eaten was Earl. Earl was very tall and thin and used to tell us she wished she were shorter. Earl would bump her head on tree branches and had to duck to enter tents. Earl, who is no longer very tall after being eaten, has a tall yellow tent she put up herself. But on some nights, she takes down all of the blankets of her tent and sleeps without a tent. This has contributed to a resurgence of open-air sleeping among the other people in the peach grove. The dinosaur who ate Earl was very tall, even taller than Earl before she was eaten. My sister does not know this because I have not written her this letter yet. I will tell her, when I write this letter, that Earl was eaten outside the peach grove while she was walking through the tall grass, looking for the new baby.

The baby was not eaten. This is good because no one knows what would have happened if the baby were eaten. No one explained to the baby that it should come back if it is eaten, so it might have gotten lost. Earl was eaten instead of the baby and everyone was very pleased. Later, someone found the baby, and David tried to explain that it should come back if eaten, but it just played with the beetles in his beard and gurgled.

There are always a few beetles in David's beard. There are no beetles in my beard. I am careful not to kiss David for more than 20 seconds at a time because that is how long it would take for a beetle to crawl from David's beard to mine. Instead, I kiss David for 19.75 seconds. When we stop kissing, I look into David's beard and see a couple of beetles peering out as if they are interested in coming to live in my beard. "No," I always tell them, "no thank you."

Earl is crying in his tent. The blanket has collapsed on him and he is a sad, crying lump under it, curled up, quivering and snorting. He is being loud. We are afraid he will attract a carnivorous dinosaur.

The baby is tugging on the blankets. Like the Calyphus that ate David, it has developed a taste for human flesh and has sensed that Earl is weak and vulnerable. But the baby has no teeth, so Earl is not in danger. Since it got lost, the baby has been known to slurp on toes that stick out of blankets at night. Because of this, we are careful to hide our toes.

I feel like I want to comfort Earl. I sit by his lumpy sad form, still covered by his collapsed tent.

The North Pole has told him that his mother is dead. He will not get to live in the North Pole with his old, strict mother. "But was she eaten?" I ask Earl. "No. She is dead," he says.

I say, "I don't know why you are so sad. She'll come back. Maybe she will come back to the peach grove to live with you, Earl."

Earl sits up and looks at me through his collapsed tent. I cannot see his face. He suddenly seems calm. He says, "No one comes back from the dead, Earl."

This doesn't make any sense to me.

Later I ask David what this means and he hands me the baby. There are beetles in its newly-grown beard, so I know David has been kissing it for longer than 20 seconds. David does not answer my question about Earl, whose mother is dead.

I am going to write to my sister in Africa and tell her what Earl said. Maybe she will be interested and send herself back with a Calyphus to answer me in person and conduct some studies for another book.

The next morning, the baby sucked a finger off of Earl's left hand. To retrieve it, David had to cut open the baby.

I am watching the baby to make sure it does not cry or die. Its big, lamp-like eyes blink slowly and deliberately. I do not know Morse code. I think it is telling me that it wants Earl's finger back. I tell it, "No, I'm very sorry, no." It blinks twice. I think that means "yes."

David bursts into the tent. Earl, whose mother is dead, has killed a Calyphus. It was the Calyphus who ate David. Enraged, David balls his hands into fists. He grabs the baby. But he did not sew it up after removing Earl's finger from its esophagus, and the baby's organs spill all over the floor. They are warm and wet and David slips in them. I take the baby, who blinks feebly one last time, and David and I run out from under the tent. As David runs, the beetles lose their grip on the hairs of his beard and slip into the air. They fly around us, swarming everywhere, and more are coming. The dead Calyphus is on the ground ahead. Earl, who has been eaten twice, is standing over it, crying like the Earl whose mother is dead cried yesterday. Earl's Calyphus is dead. It was not eaten. It will not come back from the dead.

David grabs my hand as we are running. His fingers are slippery and warm with the baby's blood, and I cannot hold onto him. The swarm of beetles grab hold of our bodies with their little two-pronged feet, and we are lifted into the air by our ears and elbows and belly buttons. We soar above the peach trees, the beetles carrying us higher and higher. The baby is slipping from my arms, but the beetles are carrying it too. It is not dead. The beetles have replaced its missing organs with other beetles and sewed it back together.

Now we are above the peach trees. Everyone on the ground is smaller than a beetle. The stegosauruses on the fringes of the peach grove are growing smaller and smaller. The carnivorous dinosaurs in the tall grass are growing smaller and smaller. The cities and buildings are growing smaller and smaller. David's slippery fingers part from mine but his face remains warm and determined. Beetles pull me away from the baby and David. The baby gurgles as it floats out of reach. I am being carried up.

I am carried high above clouds. The beetles crawl into my ears and nose. They squeeze their fat black bodies underneath my fingernails and between my teeth. They crawl into my beard and nestle under my chin. If I ever come down, I will write to my sister, EARL, and tell her about these beetles.

For now, I am being carried up. I am flying. I can no longer speak.

BULLY

Asphalt is composed mostly of crude oil. It melts slightly in the sun, and gathers in thick, fat rolls on hillsides. It is a bad paving material in hot climates.

Cement is composed mostly of sand. While it does not warp or melt under great heat, it does crack. Cement is also a bad paving material in hot climates.

But, faced with the choice, George would rather have a quick, decisive crack than a gradual, rolling distortion.

He doesn't have a say, however. His face is pressed up against asphalt. He can smell the oil. It's tangy, bitter, a little smoky. He can feel his cheek grinding against the peaks and valleys of the surface, flesh working its way off his face in stripes and chunks.

He can feel small rocks working their way under his skin, lodging in his cheek, in his eyebrow to be discovered months later when they work their way to the surface again and he digs them out in the shower. He can hear them plunk pathetically into the water pooling at his feet. Little ribbons of blood swirl around them, magically.

"Pussy!"

George closes his eyes.

***

In the summertime, Anita walks through tiers of corn and yellow bell peppers, held up by stone retaining walls, shrouded in the tendrils of wild strawberry plants and squash. She heaves a lazy rabbit up one tier and climbs up after it. Shepherd, the neighbor's Saint Bernard, growls menacingly at the end of his leash, then whines and puffs. His baggy cheeks fluff out. The rabbit takes one great leap and settles down to munch a fallen snap pea. Anita lugs the rabbit up another tier. George watches her clamber up the stone wall, her pink shoe kicking off bits of dirt and sand. There is a well-worn path through the hanging squash. The ground on the final tier is flat and dry. Pear trees, apple trees, and a cherry tree hang over them. A blueberry bush is swelling with purple fruit. The ground around the bush is black.

Shepherd's tail begins to wave back and forth, swatting the side of the dog house like a drum.

Anita looks back. George is right behind her. The rabbit takes another leap. Its black eyes close in the sun as it munches on the little piece of snap pea it took with it from the last tier.

Anita picks a blueberry. Shepherd's tail is beating out the rhythm of a Sousa. Anita feeds Shepherd a blueberry. George pets the rabbit.

***

On the bus, George sinks down in a seat near the front. He props his backpack up beside him, facing the aisle. He scrunches down, trying to make the seat look empty, except for the bag. The bag isn't big enough to shield him from view. Before any other children get on the bus, the bus driver walks down the aisle and looks at George.

"Why don't you sit in the front seat today, George?"

"No thank you, ma'am."

The bus driver taps her acrylic fingernails on the plastic seat and huffs. "Suit yourself."

Other children get on the bus. The backpack shield is working. No one is looking at him. The huge white bandage on his left cheek is facing the window. As long as he looks straight ahead no one will see it.

A fat girl with glasses sits down across the aisle.

"What's on your face?" she asks.

George's whole body flushes. "It's just a bandage," he snaps, turning pointedly away.

She looks out the window and crosses her arms.

The other boys get on the bus. The bus driver grabs one of their arms as they pass. "Hey," she says, "Behave yourself today, this is your first warning."

***

George takes a shower when he gets home. He grabs the laundry detergent from underneath the sink and pours some over his head. He scrubs his scalp until it starts to bleed. When he gets out of the shower, his hair still smells like urine.

He stares at himself in the mirror. His face looks like a slab of raw meat. There are still stripes of asphalt visible beneath the raw, pink surface. Dots of blood ooze to the surface of the scratches. A little stream of watery blood cuts his forehead in half. George puffs out his stomach and raises his arms. He tests his arm muscles and then slams his fist into the bathroom counter. "Pussy!" He grinds his fist against the white tiles. He imagines that they crack and crumble, he punches again and the counter splits in two. He punches again and the whole sink explodes. Shards of glass from the mirror explode outward. None of them hit George, they all fly straight past him, burying themselves in the faces of the other boys, who wail and cry like babies.

George combs his hair and pretends to shave his face with his dad's electric razor.

The house next door looks empty. Yellow, leaf-less cornstalks lean over on one another. The snap pea poles are bent together and tangled in string. All of the squash are gone, or rotting in mushy piles on the ground. Empty tomato cages are stacked under the pear tree. Shepherd is nowhere to be seen. The water in his bowl is a murky brown.

Rummaging through the medicine cabinet he finds gauze, Tums, and Power Ranger band-aids. He empties the box of band-aids and opens them one at a time. He sticks them to the edge of the counter in a line. When all seven band-aids are open, he sticks them together to form a long strip. He tapes the gauze to his cheek with the band-aid strip. He chews up a Tums tablet and spits it out. It tastes like cotton.

George's older sister comes home with two friends. They make sandwiches and pour out small glasses of gin from the black bottle in the liquor cabinet. They dare each other to take sips and then make faces. George sits on the carpet in the living room and watches them quietly. His sister throws a pillow at him.

"Gross, George, you're bleeding." George touches the bandage on his cheek. The band-aid strip is coming loose. The bandage is wet.

***

Anita and George are in the oldest apple tree. The neighbor is down below with a big plastic crate. He is piling apples into the crate as Anita and George shake them down. Shepherd is cowering in his dog house. "He thinks the sky is falling," the neighbor says.

"The sky is falling, the sky is falling," Anita chants, jumping up and down on a branch. Apples rain down everywhere.

George shakes another branch half-heartedly. A single

apple plops into the soft leaves below.

Anita laughs. It is a sound like cars roaring around a race-track.

***

At school, it is too windy for recess. There have been tornado warnings. They are in the gymnasium. George sifts through games in dilapidated cardboard boxes held together with tape, rubber bands, and string. Everything is missing most of its pieces. Except Snail's Pace Race. Some of the snails have been chewed on. George takes the game and crawls underneath one of the tables. He sets up the board. You are supposed to have five people to play this game, but George always plays with just himself. George rolls the dice as quietly as possible and moves the green snail forward.

One of the other boy's head appears under the table.

"What are you doing George? Are you playing a baby's game?" He laughs.

George clenches his fist around the little wooden dice as tightly as he can. The boy flips over the snail board. All five snails slide across the floor. George picks up the green snail in his other hand and looks at it. The boy stands up and aims a kick at George's shoulder. George's whole body flies forward into the bench seat on the opposite side of the table. The edge of the seat catches him in the chest. He gasps for air. The wooden dice drop from his hand and roll out from under the table.

"George!" A woman in an orange vest says, bending down to scowl at him, "Sit at the table if you're going to play with the games."

His back feels warm and prickly, like something is crawling there. He scratches it, his head down.

***

On the way to the bus, someone pushes George and he falls on the sidewalk, his hands and knees scrape against the cement. A teacher rushes forward and picks him up off the ground. It is George's old kindergarten teacher, Mrs. Jensen. She has Kanga, the kangaroo hand puppet, on her hand. Kanga's nose is in George's armpit.

"Ouch," Mrs. Jensen says, setting George on his feet. She takes Kanga off her hand and looks at her index finger. A tiny bead of blood is rising on the tip. "Something must have poked me."

George rubs his hands on his pants, leaving two red stripes.

"Better come in," Mrs. Jensen says, gesturing with Kanga to the door of her classroom.

"I'm fine," George says. He runs toward the buses before she can say anything else.

There are no free seats on the bus. George sits next to the fat girl with glasses. She scowls at him.

***

George knocks on the neighbor's door. The old man cracks open the door a little.

"Isn't it a bit cold to be outside playing, George?" he asks, opening the door wider so that Shepherd can stick his big head through the crack. Shepherd snuffs happily. "Alright, just a few minutes."

He opens the door wide and Shepherd bounds out into the yard.

George follows him around the pear trees, down the hill, around the fence, and into someone else's yard. Someone is watching from the kitchen window. George takes Shepherd's collar and tugs him back into the neighbor's yard. George breaks corn stalks and throws them for a while. Shepherd bounds after them and brings them back. When they have broken an entire stalk, the neighbor opens the door and whistles. Shepherd looks at George, then sprints back up to the door, taking each tier in a single leap. "Sorry George!" the neighbor calls.

***

He is trying to look at his back in the mirror, but he can't get a good look. He can see some of his back, he can see one side at a time, but his neck doesn't bend far enough.

When he looks over his left shoulder, the mirror George looks over his right shoulder. Everything itches.

***

The pattern on the sofa is almost completely worn away. The little velvet hairs of what was once a sort of checkerboard with flowers or animals are too sparse to make a pattern. It is just plain woven cloth now with mysterious shadows. George's legs do not reach the ground from any chair in the office. He doesn't feel any smaller than usual. The furniture was made for giants. He can see the silhouette of his sister and his mother behind the etched glass door to the vice principal's office. His mother sounds sad. His sister sounds kind. She always sounds kind when she is talking about George. They must be talking about him.

***

George is on the asphalt again. His bandage is bunched up under his eye from being dragged across the wood chips. There are splinters in his hair. They are under the slide. No one can see them. One of the boys is stepping on George's arm, the second boy is kneeling on his shoulder.

The third boy punches George right in the spine. He cries out involuntarily and all three of them punch and kick with all their might.

Someone looks out from inside, "What are you doing?"

It's an older girl. It's one of George's sister's friends. George tries to hide his face.

She disappears.

One of the boys gives George a final kick. Pain flares up in George's side, obscuring all other pain. It is the white hot master of all pain. Tears burst out of his eyes, his mouth cringes up into an almost smile-like grimace. His face flushes and he goes temporarily deaf and blind. He is levitating above arctic tundra. Everything has a sharp edge, all of the plants are covered in ice. If the wind blows, the branches will snap. George is weightless, shards of broken plant-ice are floating around him.

When his hearing returns, the boy is screaming, clutching the foot that connected with George's rib. An orange-jacketed woman appears under the slide. She shakes George's shoulder. The boy is still screaming, rolling in the wood chips.

"What did you do, young man."

The boy is screaming words, "He has a knife, he has a knife!"

George tries to prop himself up on one elbow.

***

Someone is holding his hand. It feels like Anita, but it is George's sister. They both have smooth, small fingers and little round fingernails.

George's sister lets go of his hand and runs out of the room. He is in the nurse's office, lying on a plastic bed with a crinkly white sheet of paper just wide enough to reach each of his shoulders.

The nurse's head appears around the door.

"You shouldn't fight, George. If you have a problem, find a teacher. Don't ever fight with the other students. You're lucky you're not suspended."

***

In five months, in four months and three weeks, in three months and six weeks, Anita will return.

George dreams that Anita touches his hand and begins to scream, she screams and screams, Shepherd hides in his dog house and the neighbor says, "The sky is falling."

***

When George gets off the bus, the boys follow him quietly. One of them limps on a crutch.

The bus driver looks at George questioningly. George doesn't look back.

The bus pulls away, leaving a cloud of grey smoke and a trail of white dust off the gravel road. George stands to the side and waits for the boys to pass, pretending to tie his shoe. Two of the boys pass. One of them is the one with the crutch. The third kicks George squarely in the jaw. George hits the gravel. Red stars burst in his eyes. He gasps.

The boy reaches down to grab George by his coat, then stumbles back, holding his hands out in front of him, screaming. George raises his arms and looks under them. Long, brown needles are poking through his down jacket. Feathers are floating around him.

The boy yanks long, hollow needles from each of his hands. He is crying. The ends of the needles are sharp.

The boy aims a kick at George and George flinches into a ball. The boy gets a needle in the shin. He screams again. This time he doesn't pause, but limps, crying, down the gravel road to his friends, who turn with him and run away yelling, "Freak!"

A CULTURE OF BACTERIA

• • • • • •

Fermier Johanson spreads the toes of the student. "Here," he indicated somberly, "One may see a culture of bacteria."

Fermier was simultaneously excited and disgusted by his ability to annually select from among his forty to ninety pupils, a student with a visible bacteria culture living on their person.

The student peered closely at the folds of speckled flesh in the crevice of his greater and lesser digits. "Yes," he said, "Yes I see it."

"It's revolting!" said a member of the audience.

Fermier released the foul foot and sanitized his fingers.

For lunch he had spicy thai and a banana. Indigestion interrupted his four o'clock lecture and he dismissed the class (to great fanfare) twenty-five minutes early.

His wife called the office at half-past six and told him she was having dinner with Paco. Paco lived down the street. Fermier paid Paco thirty dollars to cut the front grass every week, which took Paco less than ten minutes. Technically, Paco made more money for his time than Fermier ever would. Fermier did not find this emasculating. His wife talked about Paco incessantly. On the phone, she told him she was going to a movie with Paco after dinner and that he should not expect her home until three at the earliest.

"It's a long movie," Fermier said.

"It's foreign," his wife replied.

At seven o'clock, the humanities secretary knocked on his door and jangled her keys in his face. "Locking up," she said. Her fetid, diseased breath wafted across the office, constricting the airflow and causing his lungs to balloon out in panic. The secretary had advanced gingivitis. Fermier gagged. The secretary's husband (Rich) had left her last September for a bulimic social worker. Rich and the social worker had traveled to India together from whence they sent postcard photographs of themselves holding skeletal children and building small houses. The secretary bought a turtle and named it Rich. Fermier imagined that, when she was alone, the secretary would turn Rich (the turtle) on his back and prod his soft underbelly with the sharpened point of a pencil while his legs windmilled slowly and hopelessly. Technically, Fermier thought, it was better to revenge oneself on a turtle than a man. On the screensaver of the secretary's computer was a close-up photograph of Rich (the turtle) and the secretary, nose to nose. Fermier washed his face and hands vigorously in the faculty restroom before leaving for the night.

Not wanting to be seen by any students, he avoided the main campus walk.

But behind the theatre building, the student whose toes Fermier had displayed to the class earlier in the day approached him. "Hey Professor Johanson," the student said, grinding the twisted butt of a cigarette into the thigh of the bronze Native American he had been leaning against, "That was cool, what you showed us in class with the thing in my toes, you know?"

Fermier nodded, trying to look as busy and important as possible.

The student was addicted to painkillers. He had been in and out of rehabilitation centers periodically throughout the last four years. That is where he picked up the habit of chain-smoking. The student usually relapsed while enrolled in Fermier's remedial biology course. Fermier felt the sudden urge to tell the student that painkillers were technically less harmful to his body than unfiltered, hand-rolled cigarettes.

The student held out his hand. Fermier shook it. Walking away, Fermier tried to wipe his palm clean on the backs of his khaki colored business slacks.

Miniscule bacterial spores had lighted on his pink, clammy phalanges. They reproduced.

Fermier drove home in relative silence. At a stoplight he hummed, "Jesse's Girl" by Rick Springfield.

When he arrived at his house the lawn was freshly mown.

His wife's car was not in the driveway, it was down the street in Paco's driveway. Loud music was coming from the house. All of the bottom floor windows of the house were glowing gold and yellow.

Anger trickled down into Fermier's tingling hand. The bacterial spores began to reproduce faster. Fermier did not turn on the lights in his dark, empty house.

He turned on the faucet and was about to squirt a dollop of SoftSoap brand hand soap from the little penguin-patterned plastic dispenser when he stopped. Fermier shut off the faucet and sat down on the couch, gazing at the fingers of his hand.

Another flash of anger seeped down Fermier's arm and into his hand. The bacteria divided and dispersed.

Fermier prepared a mixture of sugar water and gelatin in a large soup pot on the stove.

When the mixture was warm, he turned off the burner and carried the pot into his bedroom. Fermier bundled the duvet into a large circle on the bed and poured the solution into the center. The gel set quickly. Finally, Fermier pressed the palm of his hand against the gelatin. It left a shallow, textured imprint.

Fermier scrubbed and sanitized his hands, the pot, the

stove, and the steering wheel of his car.

At four in the morning, Fermier's wife stumbled into the room, naked to the waist and smelling distinctly of vomit. She collapsed onto the gelatin and fell instantly asleep.

Fermier retrieved some blankets and a pillow out of the linen closet and made himself a comfortable bed on the living room couch.

When Fermier awoke, he peered into the bedroom to check on his wife. She was engulfed in a sheet of thick, mossy fur; her bare breasts had sprouted a miniature forest, bisected by a plunging, mucus-y ravine. Her hair was a misty cloud of ash, and her torso bifurcated at the buttocks into two broccoli-plumes of spongy, constantly proliferating bacteria.

THE SALMON MEN

. . . . .

When the freezing began, all of our dogs were born with wooly sweaters. In order to avoid the dangers of snagging their delicate weaves, the dogs evolved to walk upright. From higher vantages, their confidences grew and soon, in patterned sweaters and loose, stylish cashmere cardigans, the dogs became the people and the people learned to be other things.

Many tribes existed during that time. The men who were trees—who held branches aloft against the sleet—learned to still their shivers into gentle, woody quaking. The rabbit men dug holes and hibernated, hoping to sleep through to a better time. Other tribes: the grass men, the beetle men and the antelope men grew lean and small with each successive generation. But the greatest of all tribes were the salmon men. They migrated thousands of miles across the land, returning to the wilderness where all had come from. And when they arrived, they were dead. Their bodies, so smooth and quick, so iridescent and cold, were food for the earth and the frozen tundra of New Jersey was transformed into a monument of raw, pink flesh.

And in the darkest hour of our history, the bear men came. They were muscled, thick and strong, with the ancient hides of what once were real bears slung across their naked backs. Their pendulous genitalia swung out, exposed beneath the tarpaulins of bear fur like the noses of shotguns, ready to fire.

When they finally departed, only we were left, nestled up against the mountain men, too small and weak to be destroyed. But they may as well have eaten us, for what they left in their wake—in the once-lovely and fertile valley of the Salmon Men—was only dead things and sadness. We all remember them, the children especially, the ones who never saw them, or anything that they destroyed.

The mountain men have grown much larger since those days and the valley of the Salmon Men, the great and glorious forests of New Jersey, are swallowed up beneath their girth. Their feet grow deep into the rock beds and each time they give birth, an avalanche rolls down from the highest peaks, splitting the great meadows of our home in two, decimating our crops and crushing anyone too slow to outrun the boulders.

But it has been years since the last birth. As they grow larger, they are less prolific. Our meadow stretches undisturbed for miles and some say that we are the last ones here.

It has been generations since anyone saw one of our dogs. Bill tells a story of his great-grandfather's encounter with a greyhound. When Bill's great-grandfather was a boy, before the darkest hour, our old dogs used to build roads into the wild. The roads had no ending and no purpose that anyone understood, no one ever drove on them or walked on them or even looked at them much. They mostly went in big circles and the dogs would come in, clear a portion of the bracken, level the ground, lay down two thick beams of wood and pave everything in between them. The boy was wandering in the forest at that time and heard the sound of panting and swishing. Curious, he crept toward the sounds as quietly as possible. Soon he found himself peering through the fronds of a low fern at a single greyhound in an argyle patterned, close-weave sweater.

The dog was maneuvering a brick into position with its nimble forepaws. The brick slid into place. With overlong, opposable thumbs, the greyhound extracted a small spackling knife from its beige tool belt. The boy gasped, quite involuntarily, and the greyhound whipped around.

Its eyes, as the boy would later tell his own son, and his son's son, and his grandson's son, were pale gold.

Today I am walking in the forest. Tree men grow bravely where once their ancestors were slaughtered by the bear men. Wolf men howl in the distance. Rabbit men and badger men scurry to and fro in the undergrowth. A few bird men are perched in the branches of the trees. It is not difficult for a bird man to distinguish between a real tree and a tree man. This is for two reasons. Like the mountain men, the tree men have evolved to look very similar to the object of their imitation. They have deep roots, long wooden fingers and clutch handfuls of brightly colored leaves that they mostly take from other trees. But unlike the mountain men, they have not grown any bigger or stronger than their ancestors. It is because they are very scared to be eaten again by the bear men. It is hard to grow when you are afraid.

Beneath the tree men's outstretched arms I am shaded from the hot sun. It is the exact time of day when the mountain's shadow is farthest from the meadow and we are drenched in this white hot light that was once the light of the whole world. Zanzibar is walking next to me today. We are warm in the sun, underneath our slick seal-skin exteriors. When we hunt for seals, it is hard not to hunt the seal men. We cannot eat them. They are tough and stringy and their long sharp claws are forbidding. But sometimes a seal man is hunted and often times the hunted seal man is killed. No one is much bothered by the death of a seal man. Especially if someone gets to wear his skin. It would have been different in the days before, the days before our dogs were born with sweaters and everyone was a person.

Zanzibar weaves two sticks together. They are willow

73

branches. He has made a living weaving willow branches together, for this is how our homes are made.

I wonder what these branches will be when Zanzibar is finished weaving them. Maybe they will be a chair or a bureau or a handbag.

All of the handbags, bureaus and chairs in the meadow are made from willow branches. And all of the willow branches come from one willow tree. The willow tree's name is Garcia and Garcia has been here for a thousand years. Her bark is brittle and grey, the many knuckles of her are ringed with moss and rot. Garcia has a smell but it is hard to talk about the smell of her as it is the smell of willow trees and everything is made out of willow tree branches.

Zanzibar is young, his eyes are sunken down and he is much taller than the trees. Some say he was once a tree. Some say he is one of the trees that learned to be other things. Zanzibar's willow branches are at my eye level. They are twisting furiously. Then they stop. They are a dog. The dog is naked.

A coolness falls. The mountains' shadow has caught up with us and we are cold again inside our sealskin suits. Felice is running through the meadow.

A bear man. A bear man. The boys have seen a bear man. She screams, her arms and hands waving frantically toward us. Zanzibar looks at the willow branch dog and at me. He trots evenly down the hillside, his long, flat feet eating up the ground as he goes. Dirt and bits of prairie grass fly up. Felice runs toward him. Felice leaps into his running arms. They hold hands. They run toward the willow branch houses.

Sometimes boys see bear men. They are never really bear men. All the bear men are dead. All the bear men have been dead for a hundred years. Still, sometimes boys see them. It is hard to tell if a boy is lying, if a boy is scared, if a boy is smart or dumb. So always we must believe them. Just in case. It is never good to have a boy around. Boys are bad luck.

We try only to have girls in the meadow. But no known herb

can prevent a boy, though the midwife has tried so many.

But the boys, standing in tall grass with their shoes in their hands, are crying and trembling. Zanzibar is shaking one when I arrive. The boy's head lolls back and forth, his sobs come in great, spittle-y bursts. Felice shrieks nearby.

The boys have seen bear men. Outside of the meadow. On the edge of the forest. Farthest from the mountain men.

***

Later Zanzibar will tell me this: When it is difficult to remember why we do not hunt the seal men or why we do not use the tree men's fingers to weave our houses, I come here to remember that we are people.

***

It is many hours before we have decided what to do. It has been a hundred years since there were bear men here. No one remembers much about them, except that they are fierce, except that they are large, muscled, fanged, clawed, and angry. No one remembers anything about them except the various shades and colors that they come in. The shape and diameter of their muzzles. Their uncanny sense of smell. Their good eye sight. Their loud voices. Their stench.

In the time before, the time before we hunted seals and sewed them into suits, we had furs and pelts to make things. When the fur was boiled and stretched, and the scrapings sat in the sun for days beside the river, a smell would rise from the tannery. A dangerous, chemical smell. A smell we no longer smell. That is the smell of the bear men.

By the time a plan is formed, night has fallen. We light fires near the woods and station guards with long willow branches. Their seal skin suits glisten and gleam in the firelight. The women continue to cry. The boys have been tucked into their beds and gently scolded. No one in the meadow stirs.

***

In the morning we are tired, the women are still crying and the boys have been woken and gently scolded. Felice comes to me and tells me that someone has been taken. Impossible I say, looking at Zanzibar and the other men. We watched the forest all night. There was no sign of struggle, Felice says, dabbing her eyes, it was Lola.

Lola was once the smallest girl. As she grew, her mother shrunk and by the time Lola was eleven and stringy, her mother was the size of a cat. When Lola was fifteen and pink-cheeked, her mother was a dandelion. Now Lola is a woman and her mother lives in a sewing basket by the fire of their home. There is no sweeter, lovelier girl than Lola. She is the daughter of Zanzibar. She is the daughter of the meadow. She likes to wander among the mountain men. She can speak to them, when they will listen, and has spent days warming herself on their grey knuckles. If Lola has been taken by the bear men, I am afraid.

Felice brandishes the sewing basket and says, leaving her mother all alone, leaving her mother all alone.

If Lola has been taken by the bear men, I am afraid.

***

Time passes and no bear men are seen on the periphery of the meadow. The boys are gently scolded and no one sees any sign of Lola. Zanzibar walks slowly through the forest with me and I try to imagine the bear men with Lola, deep in the forest. When I imagine what horrors have been done my heart begins to shiver and I feel the hole in my chest widening, letting in cold air and my veins begin to freeze. I imagine a different scene. They are all drinking tea from willow branch cups and smiling calmly at one another.

Let me show you something, Zanzibar says in his deepest voice. I nod and he leads me to a part of the mountain men. It is a fingernail the size of a house. It is as thick as a willow tree. It is on the end of a left hand digit. It has a calcium deposit near the cuticle. No one here will remember what I am going to tell you, except you. And maybe not even you.

***

When grey clouds inch into the sky and the rain begins, flooding the meadows and rinsing off the willow tree, we call the specialist. It is Garcia. Garcia is dying. His largest branch has fallen. Green and yellow mold erupts from the severed portion, chunks of foamy wood fall out onto the ground. It is all soft and sponge-like. The whole tree is rotting. This will be the end. Everyone is anxious and sad. The specialist draws out his stethoscope and listens long and hard at the base of Garcia. He listens to the roots, to some spectators, to the rocks. He digs a hole and listens to the hole. He seems sad, like everyone else. He shakes his head. This will be the end of Garcia.

With the news that the willow tree is dying, we all start to pack our willow branch bags. We will have to go, move on to another place with a willow tree. Our willow tree cannot be the last, the only willow tree, they say. But I know that it is. I know we will never find another willow tree, even if we walk across the entire earth. Even if we all split up and search the continent inch by inch, we will not find another willow tree. This is because when a father dies, there is not another father. Even if you search the whole continent, scour every inch of the earth for a thousand years, there will never be another father.

Though looking for one is sometimes the only thing to do.

When our bags are packed and our houses are empty we look at each other. We look and look until someone gasps and points past me to the edge of the wood.

77

We whirl around. No one moves. Four bear men are standing at the edge of the forest. One is kneeling on the ground, his hands are bound and his furs are stretched back. A bare white chest shows deep, red trenches evenly scored into the skin. This bear man is crying, his chest is heaving. Beside him stands another, proudly shrouded in his bear suit. In front of them stand two more bear men, glowering at us. And in front of them, stumbling toward us, seal skin suit hanging from her shoulders in strips, her once pink-cheeked face pale, grey, and framed in lank strings of bluish hair, is Lola.

She is clutching a fluffy brown ball.

It is a bear man.

We look at Lola. Zanzibar, her father, takes a halting step toward her. He knows what we must do. Now no time is spared in discussion. Lola falls to her knees, crawls around with one arm steadying the tiny bear man, and tries to crawl back to the other bear men. The kneeling bear man wails, falls forward, beats the ground with his shoulders and struggles to free his bound-tight hands. The bear man in front roars loudly and leaps forward. Lola shields the infant bear man and pulls herself to her feet. No one is going to help her. No one is saying, this is not right.

Zanzibar takes another halting step. Our breath is held. We see him reach her and strike her down. We see him reach into the shredded remnants of her dress and pull out the brown poof that is the tiny bear man.

We will rip the bear man apart and each imbibe a little of his strength so that when the other bear men come, we can fight them. It is the reason we are still alive. It is hard to remember that once, the bear men were people like us. Before the freezing came and all our dogs were born with sweaters.

23, 28

In the evening, Marietta Galblatt was usually seen walking the perimeter of the dig with a china cup and saucer clutched before her, sipping daintily as she surveyed the work of the day.

It was a habit that some older students took to imitating, later in Galblatt's life, as a form of flattery and display of their own power.

Marietta Galblatt was no longer, by anyone's estimation, a beautiful woman. Her limp, naturally crimped brown hair was untidy and sun-bleached to the matte color of unstained wood. The formidable bosom which had, in youth, served and hindered her development as an archaeologist had been decimated by breast cancer and replaced by a featureless sloping plane. Beneath the off-white, sweat-stained undershirts of midday in the sand was a slight concavity marred by a pale, horizontal scar. In equal cruelness, time had greatly exaggerated her once voluptuous hips into doughy planets pinched and pockmarked by ample cellulite reserves. But Galblatt had retained, beneath a fairly unwrinkled brow, the fathomless, passionate black eyes that had once bewitched the President of the University of Santa Barbara and landed her the single most coveted position in archaeological research.

Years later, when the very same President had swept her off her feet and made wild love to her on their secret honeymoon/groundbreaking dig in West Africa, other candidates had called foul play, which resulted in the President's sacking on grounds of immorality, his subsequent clinical depression, and eventual suicide.

It was unfair to say, however, that Galblatt was not attractive in her way. The numerous pains and trials of her comparatively short life had never bowed her muscular shoulders and as she walked the perimeter of the dig site with the haughty grace and pride of those who have known exceptional beauty, it was clear to the students and researchers watching carefully from the tents, through the steam and smoke rising from the pots on their fires, that Galblatt wielded a power of almost unnatural attraction.

They all, without exception, wanted to be near her, liked by her, and like her. People obeyed her, instinctively.

When she returned to her own three-sided tent she was surprised to see a dark young man sitting in her chair by the tiny, crackling fire. Out here in the desert, it was unnecessary to keep a fire lit the whole night for warmth. The earth radiated heat long into the dark hours and no more was needed than a small cooking fire in the evenings to keep away the insects before the workers lay back on their blankets and fell into what was usually a deep and restful sleep.

"Excuse me," Galblatt said patiently, "I don't take students after tea." She meant to sound forbidding, but not rude. The young man did not rise or even look at her as she walked past the fire into the tent.

Galblatt picked up her notebooks and settled onto the edge of the hanging cot, her face bent away from the boy.

There was silence in the tent apart from the rustle of Galblatt's notebook pages and the gentle crackle of the fire, which within several minutes had died down to embers, casting the figure in the chair into deep, orangey shadow. Galblatt stared fixedly at the mostly shadowed face and for the first time felt a chill as the hairs on the back of her neck stood.

Eventually, Galblatt coughed loudly and said, "I don't mean to be rude, but whatever you've got to say can wait until the morning, I never take students after tea."

The figure was still. Galblatt was on the point of rising, had said, "I said," rather angrily despite the prickling fear at the nape of her neck, when, haltingly, the boy stood.

He could not have been more than a boy for, when he stood, he came barely level with the scar on her chest.

Standing, she could see his arms and his chest were abnormally large, too large for a young boy. Shoulders hunched, he let out a racking, grating cough. His collared shirt was flapping open and his shadow, on the canvas of the tent behind him, cast by the flickering fire, was wavering wildly. His hands ended in long, coiling, fleshy strings instead of fingers. The fleshy strings, like thick noodles, waved toward her.

"23, 28," he said.

He turned and walked out of the tent.

Galblatt stood still a moment, then walked after him, "What the hell?"

But he was already gone. Galblatt's narrowed eyes swept the darkness and the flickering light from dying fires around the campsite. "Hey!"

No one answered. Galblatt called again.

A man stuck his head out of a nearby tent, "Is something wrong, Doctor? Scorpion?" the man asked, clambering out of his pup tent and dusting sand off his shorts.

"No," said Galblatt, "come here a moment, Perkins."

Perkins stepped forward anxiously.

"Do we keep an older boy here, from the city?"

"Older? What age?"

Galbatt had absolutely no idea how to gauge the age of a living child, although she could tell the age of a dead one from no more than a kneecap.

She waved her hand at the height the boy had come to, "This big," she said.

"Ah, no, they're all about this big," Perkins laughed, waving his arm a half foot lower than hers.

He saw that she was not smiling and coughed awkwardly. "All the boys are seven or eight, once they've hit ten the villagers won't let them come out, they've got their own chores."

Galblatt huffed. "Might have been eight, seemed much older and anyway, he was sitting by the fire. Don't we have a tent for them?"

Perkins scratched his head, "That's odd, mum, we do —" he gestured south, "that way."

Galblatt turned without another word and, from the edge of her tent said, "Goodnight, Perkins."

"Goodnight, Doctor."

Marietta Galblatt sat gingerly on the hammock in her ember-lit tent. What a strange trick of the light, those noodle-fingers.

23, 28. 23, 28. Ages? Times? 1923? 1928? 1923, Carter enters the Tutankhamen tomb. The Roman ruins at Wroxeter in Shropshire are excavated. First dinosaur egg — Andrews in Mongolia. First Tanager expedition. 1928? Penicillin, Griffith's Experiment substantiates DNA, Dunand excavates the Byblos spatula. Ugarit is unearthed. Year 23 AD: nothing. Year 23 BC: nothing. 23000 BC: nothing.

Galblatt tore through the names and dates in her memory, searching for anyone born or deceased those years, any important event. Perhaps they weren't years and anyway, why would an Egyptian kid, whose schools probably didn't even teach Western history, be cryptically referencing the Wroxeter dates?

23: the ninth prime, number of human sex chromosomes, the atomic number of Vanadium. Vanadium. Random. Galblatt couldn't think of a single important use for or product of Vanadium, it wasn't even measurable in most of the fossils and specimens she dealt with.

28: second perfect number. Not a prime. Nickel. Nickel? Galblatt lay back and stared at the ceiling. The average length of a menstrual cycle: 28 days. The time it takes for concrete to dry: 28 days.

2328? What was happening in 2328 BC: Humanity is still sitting in the Indus Valley, Akkadian Empire. Sixth Dynasty of Egypt.

The sequence: 2. 3. 2. 8. Twice the first, halved minus one. No, no sequence.

Galblatt scribbled the numbers on a journal page, rolled over in the hammock, and fell asleep at once.

***

That night Marietta Galblatt dreamed of spaghetti. Piles of spaghetti, noodles stretching out into the distance as far as the eye could see. She knew she was standing on the brink of evolution. Primordial earth was raging and broiling all around her. Only everything was made of noodles. Noodle mountains rose in the distance, a noodle ocean swept noodle waves up onto the noodle shore. Noodles coiled around her boots, they waved around her legs and in the distance, noodle trees sprouted noodle leaves and a speckling of noodle fungus. Then a noodle cloud descended from the noodle sky toward the shore. Marietta followed it, running through the noodle, her boots squishing beneath her. A meatball rolled casually out of the noodle ocean and came to rest on the noodle shore. The huge noodle in the sky reached toward the meatball, and spaghetti sauce spilled down upon it. Marietta woke up, sweating, in her tent. She lit a lamp and made a strong cup of tea.

***

The next day was stressful. The camera crew on loan from a film studio in Cairo, while the National Geographic's people went back to cut and edit the first three episodes of a "Finding the Bible" holiday special, slipped into an underground cavern the entrance of which Galblatt's team was just beginning to excavate. They damaged the stonework, the floor, and the ceiling and while trying to extricate themselves, decimated three of their six cameras and two mic booms.

Galblatt spent the morning yelling herself hoarse at the film crew, at the student who had laid the tape around the site, and at anyone who would come close enough.

During mid-afternoon break, Galblatt called over all of the village boys and stared them each in the face until they cried. Exercising this sort of power made her feel a little less miserable, but not finding the boy she'd caught in her tent just brought back all of her frustration of the night before with the numbers 23 and 28.

That afternoon as she was making the rounds to all of the excavation sites within the perimeter, Galblatt overheard a Graduate student dictating notes. "At 23 north by eighteen minutes 47.75 seconds, 30 east by 3 minutes 57 seconds."

Galblatt paused.

"You," she said to the boy who was taking the dictation, snatching him up by the collar of his shirt. He scrambled out of the hole and inclined his head.

"Yes, Doctor?"

"Let me see your notes." His hand trembled anxiously as he extended the notes he had just taken down.

"We're just south of the city, historically, although with tectonic shift, we may be right on top of the site..." continued the student in the hole. The boy looked anxiously at the notebook.

Galblatt leafed through it until she found the coordinates. "23 degrees, she muttered."

The graduate poked his head out of the hole. "Excuse me, Dr. Galblatt, I didn't know you were here. Do you want to see the progress?"

Galblatt huffed and shoved the notebook back into the waiting hands of the undergrad.

"Go on, then," she said gruffly, waving her hand.

The grad student began rattling off the progress they had made in inches and his own speculations about the site, which had probably once been the food cellar of a house. Galblatt knew that grad students enjoyed this immensely, and listened patiently, not taking in a word of what he was saying. She was thinking about plotting 23 by 28 in her tent, she was sure that was somewhere in the desert, a little south of where they were now, miles from anything. Maybe another site.

"Excellent work, there, keep it up, you better put in a platform if you get anything under four feet. Don't want someone putting a foot through a jar."

The student beamed proudly.

Galblatt preferred working with students to other professionals. When they were dispersed like this, Galblatt always took her pick of students first and let the other archaeologists have the majority of the professionals. The other archaeologists on the site were about fourteen miles away outside of Mut, Egypt with a team of forty-five. Galblatt found she had more control over the dig when her subordinates were groveling at her feet for grants and scholarships, rather than obsessing about their own careers and conducting petty schemes to work on the best digs.

Galblatt had found, in her forty years in the field, that archaeologists were some of the vainest and most dangerous people in existence.

She stepped away from the student and wound her way back through the various patches of indented ground. The sponsors of the expedition had them excavating what was believed to be a small aesthetic settlement of around the third century, such as the one that may have been home to Saint Anthony. It was certainly Persian, pre-Muslim, but more likely an Alexandrian village on the trade route. The time was right for aesthetics, but the deep rooms, the small amount of artifacts, the huge stable being excavated by Perkin's team, pointed to a trade-route settlement, not a religious settlement.

And even if it was religious, the chances that it had any relation to Saint Anthony, an almost completely fictional character, were astronomical. The people funding a huge portion of the excavation were preying on the inanity of their viewers. Galblatt had trouble understanding why people who were purported to believe that faith requires no substantiation would fork out so much money to substantiate their faith. During her illness people urged and demanded that she pray - take solace in God. Even doctors, educated men who shouldn't have subscribed to such tripe, told her that her recovery was "in God's hands." But Galblatt never succumbed to the futile and honestly tragic worship of an imaginary deity. When the President died, Galblatt moved through what she knew to be natural, logical and not unimportant stages of grief. But none of these included self-delusion. In a world of science, mathematics, and reason, religion had no real application.

Some years ago, Galblatt had been suspended from a site for inciting aggressive behavior when she encouraged her students to call the sponsor's "Search for the Word" project dangerously childish and naïve on camera. After this experience, declaring that the archeology field was becoming more and more puritanical, Galblatt had trained herself to be more reserved. She was opposed to illogical behavior, fundamentally, so she couldn't help slipping up and rolling her eyes at the television crews and their ludicrously earnest hosts crawling into pre-Egyptian burial caverns saying: "Noah's ark is likely preserved in a mound of earth such as this."

Codswallop.

She had been on bad terms with the administration of the college ever since. Mut was, more or less, banishment. The last stop in a series of miserably underfunded, unscientific excursions where the chances of uncovering anything of value to her research were null. She wouldn't admit it yet, but the college was slowly pushing her out.

***

Galblatt finished her rounds at a jog, glancing disinterestedly into the partitioned squares around the main foundation, and returned to her tent. She untied the dusty tent flaps and let them fall together behind her, blocking out the harsh sun.

It was musty and stiflingly hot inside the tent. She went to the wooden chest in the corner and withdrew a battered map of the area. Galblatt preferred the paper maps, she had literally hundreds of every sight she had ever excavated. There were computerized maps and GPS-enabled charting equipment at all the sites, but the computers failed to conjure up an actual image of a place that people lived. Half of an archaeologist's work was intuition of human behavior and if Galblatt couldn't imagine humans behaving in a place, she couldn't tell people where to dig.

She followed a line down from the top of the map and pressed her forefinger into the exact point of intersection between longitude 23 and latitude 28.

The point was only twenty miles from the camp.

"Boy!" she yelled loudly. A wiry little boy the color of an Anjou pear appeared at her elbow instantly. "Get me a camel."

***

Loping across the hot desert sand, Marietta Galblatt cursed the domestication of the camel. What a terrifically odorous, useless beast. The camel snorted and spat as if it knew exactly what she was thinking. Its keening moan was like the death cry of a falling albatross.

Galblatt's request for an expedition party had been denied. Actually, the curator (visiting from Mut) had laughed in her face and turned his back without response. Galblatt had taken this as a rejection. She considered hijacking a pair of young boys but feared the talk. Well, she had reasoned, they couldn't punish her for taking *herself* forty-seven miles into the desert.

The air was barely cool enough to breathe. Everything that touched her skin burned her: a flap of cloth, a bit of sand, the prickly-feathered end of her sun-bleached ponytail.

Around midday the camel began to make dying sounds. "What is wrong with you!" Galblatt screamed as the animal bowed underneath her. The ground rushed up and she wriggled free before the camel could topple over onto her. She scuttled across the scalding sand as the animal leaned dangerously, swayed, righted itself, and fell. Even from its knees, the fall was a substantial distance, dust and sand billowed out from its massive, ugly body. "A faulty animal!" Galblatt screamed again, "Gave me a faulty animal." But there was no one there to hear her. She was a good four hours from the camp, so much farther from actual civilization.

Galblatt sat for a while. The sand directly beneath her was cool, everything else burned. The heat waves off the desert sand were making her sea-sick. She stared. No, it wasn't heat waves. Something was twisting around on the horizon. It was a long, fleshy finger. It was beckoning.

Galblatt blinked, closed her eyes. The finger was projected in reverse on the hot pink insides of her eyelids. Beckon. Beckon.

She opened her eyes again and it was still beckoning. It was more definite now, a finger, a long, flat finger. Like a noodle, wobbly and flaccid, waving around on the horizon. But it ended in heat waves, she couldn't see where it connected to a hand, or an arm, or a body.

She was relatively sure she was hallucinating. She tried to ignore it. She pulled her tent out from under the camel and draped it over her, thinking she'd sleep until night and then walk back to camp in the dark. There was no way she was getting there in the middle of the day. Best to sleep through the heat.

***

Years ago, Marietta had wandered off into the desert, out of the camp. She remembered the dizzying panic when she was out of sight of the camp and completely directionless. She had stormed off after an argument with the President and, in an area almost identical to this, she'd finally stopped walking and realized she had no idea where she was. There had been a long hill which seemed to wave back and forth. It wasn't a dune, it had a structure beneath the sand, rock or an old section of a fallen wall. The actual placement of the sun was impossible to discern, the whole sky was a blinding whiteness. She was dehydrated, and the complete silence pressed in on her. No wind, no insects, no sand tinkling over sand. Silence.

She walked up to the top of the hill and collapsed. Under the burning sand, in Marietta's dreams, a huge twisting arm had lain, petrified, the once soft, rounded arm of some squid-like creature of incomprehensible proportions. In her dreams, the handless arm curled around her, cradling her like an infant as she slept, and when she woke, night had fallen and the only interruption of the clearest, fullest, most intense night sky of her entire life was the blur of firelight in the west: the camp. The arm seemed to point toward it, toward the President, asleep in his tent. And by the time Marietta stumbled back into the camp, ragged and blistered by the sun the President, from the back of a camel, was radioing a helicopter to search the perimeter, preparing to embark himself on a rescue mission to find her. It was dawn and the sky was pink. And she loved him.

***

Galblatt awoke. The change in temperature had been rousing her for a long time. Her eyelids snapped open. She could feel the heat from the earth, but no heat from the sky. She threw off the tent and took a look at the camel. Still dead.

But on the horizon was a light. The weird thoughts of the first expedition with the President must have affected her brain. There was no way she was still within sight of the camp. She checked the compass by the bright starlight. And, indeed, if she had started out in the right direction, the light was in the opposite direction of the camp.

Galblatt paused. At best, it was another dig site, preferably conducted by some nation whose language she spoke. Hopefully at 23, 28. At worst… what? Who else would be out here? Thieves? Pirates?

What were the chances of that?

Probably some nomadic tribe with water, food, and transportation. Galblatt never kept local currency on her, but they might trade for the tent, for canteens, for the camel's carpet. She quickly stripped the animal, tied everything she could up in a pack and slung it over her back.

The light was not far off, maybe three hours, or four. She quickened her pace. The pack cut into her shoulders.

The ground was well-lit by the stars, everything was pale blue. After an hour she was making good time. The light was burning hugely, bigger than a fire, it must be a city. But what city was out here, in the middle of the Sahara… almost literally?

Not a city that Galblatt knew of. Not a city with a telephone.

She kept walking. The straps of the pack bent her shoulders forward. Sweat trickling down her arms felt like icy fingers stroking her flesh. Her knees kept buckling beneath her, plunging her into the sand. Thirst and muscle fatigue made her shiver. Eventually Galblatt was close enough that she should have been able to distinguish houses or tents but there was nothing except wide, soft tendrils of light, emanating from what looked like a single, tall, jagged dune against an otherwise gently rolling horizon.

Blinded by the bright light, she crawled across the sand toward the mountain.

The surface of the hill was lumpy and vaguely porous… like a knot of tree roots covered in plastic.

And then Marietta Galblatt realized what she was looking at. The sun was paling the eastern sky. And she realized how long she must have been traveling. That she was at 23, 28.

***

It was a monstrous pile of spaghetti; each waving noodle iridescent with light.

Galblatt hoisted herself up off the sand and dropped the heavy pack she had dragged across the desert to this spaghetti mountain. She was struck by the pointlessness of having brought it along. And she took a final step toward the mountain.

A noodle shot toward her and seemed to prod her in the chest with its huge tentacle. This, surely, was the reason she had been called to 23, 28. The reason she had been visited by the noodle boy, the reason she had argued with the curator and gone off alone. The reason she had been able to hike these twenty miles into the desert on foot. She felt her chest expand with pride and happiness.

***

The noodle shape seemed to rise as well. Galblatt thought of her frenzied description to the President of the mound she had slept on in the desert. She remembered the beads of sweat breaking over her eyebrows as she tried feverishly to plot exactly where she had been. Faithful, believing, the President had sent out parties, had sent out the rescue helicopter to look at the area. The chances of finding anything in the untraveled waste of the desert, where no one went but pirates and those horrendous nomadic people, all twisted into leprous shapes as they pulled themselves through the barren landscape, were impossible. Any hint was worth investigation. But Galblatt took the effort as a pledge of affection.

The President's assistants told her, pulling her roughly aside, that he was not interested in her, but what she might have found in a sun-drunk stupor. He had not been going out to save her, but to save the college a tremendous lawsuit.

Their words rolled off her while the parties spread across the desert, searching for the hill. But the search returned nothing. There was nothing in the radius she may have traveled from the camp. She had hallucinated, misjudged, let him down, let them all down.

***

But here. Here, at 23,28, she was standing on the shape, that sand-backed, dome-topped wall she was so sure she had seen. The noodle that had prodded her withdrew into its rolling mass of light shapes. Galblatt squinted, trying to make out the texture of the rock face that supported this massive dune. It was not a wall, but an actual dome. It was completely round. Sand was shifting off the sides, the massive noodle creature's weight was unearthing the structure. It was the top two thirds of an almost perfect sphere, pockmarked, like a meatball. A petrified meatball.

Galblatt tumbled backward off the now bare structure and landed, face-down, in the rough sand. The light dimmed. The creature was gone.

***

She could hear the sounds of scraping metal and laughter. The light disappeared leaving Galblatt sun-blinded, blinking back tears of surprise and exhaustion. Her sun-burnt eyelids crinkled painfully. Real lights, the lights of gas lamps, were shining around her. A generator was humming coolly some ways away and the laughter, sounding more and more familiar, was coming from a glowing white tent surrounded by a cluster of smaller, rattier tents. A large mismatched herd of camels, horses and some out-of-place looking mules were tied outside the cluster of tents. Some were standing, some kneeling on the ground. Galblatt felt a twinge of annoyance and regret, remembering the camel that had been sacrificed to bring her here. But where was here?

Galblatt moved toward the camels, they grunted and bayed in annoyance at her approach. Packs of supplies littered the ground around them, some still bore their ragged saddles and trappings. Galblatt lifted the flap of a bag. Guns. Three semi-automatics and a nest of pistols. Another bag, guns. Guns, guns, some dried meat of some sort, a large cache of passports, wallets, two thick wads of American one hundred dollar bills, what looked like a tool set, and guns.

Terrorists? Bandits? Galblatt whirled around, a jolt of fear interrupting the feeling of peace which had settled on her since the encounter with the noodle creature. She briefly contemplated pocketing one of the wads of bills, for bartering purposes. But, considering all of the guns, she decided against it. The laughter rolled out of the tent again. It was familiar, distinctively familiar, laughter.

She crept into the cluster of tents.

"Now that he's dead," someone said. Galblatt strained her ears, pressing up against a tent not far from the larger, lighted white tent in the center. They were speaking English, these people. They were pirates. Desert pirates.

"What we'll need," a man said, "What we'll need is someone who knows their way around the camps. We need someone who knows how to take charge, a… you know… a leader."

"That's right, someone to keep these people in line. Someone organized."

"Pass the rum, captain," said another, "Argh."

That laughter again. It was dawn and the sky was pink. And Galblatt knew, quite suddenly, that the laughter sounded a lot like the President.

And she cleared her throat outside the door of the tent.

MOUNTAINS IN THE FURNACE

. • . • . • .

We have mountains in the furnace.

It's difficult to explain to company, why we can't turn on the heat in the house. "Well, there's a problem with the furnace" is what we usually say. We don't like to lie. But it's hard to say: "There's a delicate mountain ecosystem in the furnace," or "Our furnace is protected by the N.G.P.A. Commission," or "Turning on the furnace would result in the complete obliteration of more than 80 animal species, 250 species of plants, and innumerable varieties of insect found nowhere else." You can't just say, "There are over 1,000 acres of mountain forest located inside our furnace," to normal, god-fearing people.

Over the years we've used a lot of excuses: "The boys prefer the cold," "Cutting back on electricity bills," "Furnace needs repair." Sometimes people are pretty suspicious. They ask a lot of questions. But we found out a long time ago that it's no use telling them the truth, although sometimes we've wanted to, they only want to see it for themselves. But too much foot traffic in the forest disrupts the undergrowth and the government officials that stop by periodically to take photographs and record data about the forest get fussy about damaged plant life.

So we can't tell our guests the truth about the mountains in the furnace.

The mountains do technically belong to us, that's the strange thing about the N.G.P.A Commission, the land is protected, but still in our possession. There are pretty strict limits on what we can do in the furnace.

Apart from fishing a little in the streams, and walking in the meadows, we aren't allowed to do anything that could affect the plants or wildlife.

The government officials gave us permission to cull a herd of mischievous elk in 1992 – that was the spring when all the new growth along the river banks was being ripped up by an overpopulation of elk because almost no wolf-cubs had survived the previous year. All because of a late frost in the spring of '91.

It just goes to show you how fragile everything in nature is – how everything is connected.

We had elk in our freezer for three winters and that was with the huge barbecue we had for all of our friends at my brother Sam's house. Sam and I had quite a time getting those elk out of the furnace once we'd shot them. We had eight, overall.

The summer Sam and I taught the boys to fish, the trout count dropped below acceptable levels and we got in a lot of trouble with the government officials. Our oldest boy, Eric, turned out to be a natural fisherman. He had an eye and a hand for it that not even Sam had ever had.

Mauve and I spend a lot of time in the furnace now that the boys are grown. We climb in when the weather's nice in there and sit in the meadow in those old lawn chairs, just holding hands, reading or talking.

In our younger years we explored a lot of the western side of the mountain range – we hiked up and down, taking different routes every time, we summitted the three peaks, and kept a close eye on the wildlife. It got to the point, over the years, that all the animals knew us, even the birds would land on our hats or shoulders, looking to be fed.

Now the only hiking we do is a few miles up the mountain to this little stream where Sam and I can fish and Mauve can write and soak her feet.

When we bought the house – it was a real find. We'd wanted desperately to stay in the city, close to the hardware store where I'd worked since Mauve and I met, but Mauve was pregnant with our first son, Eric, and we needed a place to start the family right. Our realtor showed us the house right off, said it'd been on the market for about a year. It was ancient, built at the turn of the last century, but it'd been well cared for, and it was close to the city. I had just been promoted to assistant manager, and Mauve had inherited a bit of money from an aunt. We didn't really have the money for the house, but between the little extra coming in from the hardware store and Mauve's inheritance, we were able to scrape together enough to get the place.

Sam and I did a lot of work on the house the first month or so, tore up carpets and replaced wires and light fixtures. It was a hot spring, and a hot summer and there wasn't a night until October when we needed to turn on the furnace.

When we did, eventually, we found the switch disconnected. I thought I could fix it right up but Mauve thought we should call a repair guy, just in case. The thing was just as ancient as everything else there and she wanted to make sure it wasn't going to burn down the house. I didn't think it was anything I couldn't repair, but she was eight and a half months pregnant, so I humored her.

I mean, it's lucky I did.

That repair guy opened the furnace up and there it was, a whole mountain landscape, stretching off into the distance in every direction.

Of course we explored the place and called the realtor. We even called the company that had made the furnace, but no one could tell us anything about it.

A few months after Eric was born, the N.G.P.A officials

97

showed up and gave us a lot of paperwork and pamphlets.

Mauve was worried we'd have to claim the property in our taxes but, as it takes up only around two square feet, and it's inside the house, no one's ever told us we need to claim it.

We've never had heat in the house, but we've gotten used to cold winters.

At first Mauve wanted to move – after we found the mountains and there was the risk that repairing the furnace would incinerate everything inside it, our only choices were to live with it or move. We eventually decided to tough out the winters. Some years were harder than others.

But in the end it's been worth it to have the mountains, for ourselves and for the boys. From as early as either of them could walk, they'd spend days and weeks exploring the woods and meadows. Growing up with mountains in the furnace has made them strong, independent, and confident. It still strikes me, when they visit, that those boys know the forest better than the backs of their hands.

We don't regret keeping the house, or the cold in the winter. Mauve and I don't regret a thing about our lives here, in the house, and the mountains.

And Eric and his wife, Marie, just moved into a little studio apartment downtown, not far from the house, it's a real small place but it's cheap and it's just right for them. It's about eleven o'clock at night when he calls up Mauve, we're out watching the stars in the furnace and he says, "Hey Mom, our stove's broken, and we're gonna call the landlord in the morning, but Marie's just opened the thing up, and there's an ocean in there."

WIVES OF POOR MEN

·   ·   ·   ·   ·

When Melanie Edmonton walked up the stairs to the loft, the last thing she expected to find was Ernie McLeesh, her husband's college dorm mate, being absorbed by the bedpost.

They didn't really use the loft room much. When Harold had to quit the canning job because of his knee, before the office job, which was before the roof-laying job, they moved to the bedroom downstairs so that he could get around easier during the day. He spent most of that time sleeping, watching porn, and eating through three bags of nacho cheese Doritos every day. The four-poster was too hard to dismantle, and Melanie was going to have to do it alone, so they left it up there.

Ernie moaned.

It looked like he was trying to reemerge from the wood grain, his skin stretching around where his cheek met the post. Ernie was a thin man, but he looked thinner, wasted and grey. Although maybe that was the wood grain, extending out from the post, wrapping around his neck and naked shoulders.

"Hey Ernie," Melanie said. She had only come up for the broom. The floors were covered in dog hair. She was just sweeping.

She grabbed the broom, turned around and walked back down the stairs.

Sam, Ernie's wife, stopped by around noon. Melanie gave her a cup of Lipton tea and they talked about Harold, about Cyril and Judy, the latest couple at the couple's reading group, which Melanie had attended alone, every week for the last year and a half.

Melanie talked into her tea, which smelled grassy, a little like an armpit. She snorted half-heartedly.

Sam made a lot of exasperated sounds, rolled her eyes, sloshed the tea when she gesticulated.

"Unemployment," said Sam. "Thank god."

"No kidding," said Melanie. "Until that life insurance plan comes through."

"Did you get those documents in the mail?" said Sam.

"Not yet," said Melanie. "Did you?"

Sam rummaged in her huge, worn hemp purse and pulled out an unevenly folded piece of paper with calligraphic script across the top. "Do you have a…" Sam gesticulated with the papers, smacking her gum in her front teeth emphatically.

"Yeah sure," said Melanie. She dug a piece of wax paper out of the garbage piled up around the trashcan in the corner. She handed it to Sam, who spit her gum into it and shoved it into her purse.

"Anyway, I've got to pick up Roger from school." Sam rolled her eyes.

Melanie swirled her tea. The green-brown dredges stuck to the edges of the cup in a wavy line, like a W.

Sam stood up. "Remember what we said, Melanie."

Melanie nodded, still looking into her tea. "Better dead than alive."

Later that night, Sam opened the chest of drawers in the guest room. A pair of blue-green eyes blinked up at her from the back of the drawer, behind the off-white towels and dishrags. The pupils were almost completely masked by the cheap

100

tan plywood wood grain.

"Good riddance, Harold," she said, "Good riddance."

HIBERNATION

· • · · • ··

On Tuesday afternoon, after weeks of worrying about her fifteen-year-old son, Martha decided it was time to go into his room.

For months, the boy had scarcely been seen, but the effects of his presence were evident: plates and cups accumulated around the kitchen, unwashed forks and knives appeared in the bathroom sinks, clothes showed up in the laundry room. Food disappeared almost faster than she could buy it. Notes were slipped under the door, about one a week, asking for certain grocery items, most often "more pizza pockets please," and "not enough pizza pockets for tomorrow. more please." Every night around three in the morning, the second step on the stair creaked ominously and Robert's door clicked shut at the end of the hall. Other than these brief telling signs, Robert, Martha's son, could have disappeared altogether.

The women at the knitting club, all much older and more experienced in these matters than Martha, assured her that this was a phase.

"Young men go through a period in their lives when they just want to be apart from their families. It's a good sign, he's forging his own identity."

"It's best to give them their space, if you crowd him now, you're putting your relationship on the line."

"He probably has a girlfriend."

Martha was extremely skeptical of this. Robert had never shown the slightest interest in women. He was, she thought, still too young to be involved with anyone.

He did have his friends, but until recently they had always come over en masse in the daylight hours, walking through the gardenias, eating everything in sight, tracking mud and other debris into the house, leaving their tremendous sneakers in unlikely and unpleasant places. Robert had video games and a couch. And for this reason, he was quite popular.

But lately, the unearthly quiet in the daytime, the bare, hushed whispers at night, and the early morning departures...

This was a whole different sort of situation.

Martha tried approaching Luke about the problem. But Luke was, as always, unhelpful.

"He probably got a job. He's probably selling Meth. Like all the kids his age. Reprobates."

"Luke, dear, don't you think we should talk to him?"

"Why? So his pimp can come to our residence and shoot us? What's the use?"

"Then, at least we should call the police."

"Police!" Luke scoffed. "Bumbling simpletons. One more year and the kid'll be out of our hands anyway. Why cause trouble now."

"Luke, he's only fifteen."

Luke waved his hands around mockingly, "Luke, he's only fifteen!"

The previous Wednesday, Martha had woken from an undisturbed night of sleep to a clean kitchen and four unopened boxes of Pizza Pockets in the freezer.

"That's odd," she murmured. She fed the cat, watered all of the plants, rearranged the pile of papers and garbage on the kitchen table to no great effect, put in a load of laundry and turned on the television. Wednesday was Martha's day off from tutoring. On the weekends, Luke (and previously Robert) required attention and entertainment. On Wednesdays, Martha could do whatever she wanted. She usually spent the day watching television, folding laundry, and reading magazines. At four o'clock she went out for ice cream. When Robert was a boy, Martha would pick him up at school early every Wednesday and they would get ice cream together. Robert's favorite flavor was vanilla. How could a boy that likes vanilla ice cream be selling meth? Meth was for pistachio ice cream lovers, or the kids who liked clown cones.

The phone rang. It was an automated message from Robert's school telling her that her son "Row-bear-t," had missed "one, two, three, or more classes" today, "Wednesday, January fourth."

Martha hung up the phone and sat back down on the couch. She wondered if she would even recognize her son if she saw him in the street. She thought about the last time she had seen him. Sprinklings of facial hair were appearing on his chin. He was getting taller and thinner, losing all of his round, childish pudginess. He was as tall as her now, only a few inches shorter than his father. They had gone out for Luke's birthday. The whole night Luke was in a bad mood because the price of gas had gone up eleven cents from the previous day. At dinner, Robert coyly pretended to sneak sips of Martha's wine. They ordered the same thing at the same time from the waiter and laughed for a full five minutes. He told a lewd joke, made a mozzarella stick dance, flicked peanut shells at the loud people in the booth next to them, and he gave his father a floppy green fishing hat and a handmade card that read "You're the best, Dad," in Robert's sloppy, nearly illegible child-of-the-computer-age handwriting.

Robert might have a full beard now. Martha imagined coming home and finding a bearded terrorist in her kitchen, eating pizza pockets out of a cereal bowl, surrounded by dirty dishes.

She walked upstairs, stared at Robert's closed bedroom

door, gathered the clothes from outside of the door, and took them downstairs. She buried her face in the clothes. They smelled dirty, like a pubescent boy who still hasn't developed the habit of showering regularly. There were no foreign smells, no cigarette smoke, no mysterious and unfamiliar perfumes. No meth lab smell. What did a meth lab smell like?

Martha wandered into their bathroom. She rummaged through Luke's bathroom drawer. There was the card. It was only four months ago. It didn't seem like a long time, but then, Martha supposed, to someone who has only been alive for fifteen years, four months is a long time.

At knitting group that evening, Martha was distracted. Her sweater was beginning to look like a sea creature. Betty put a hand on her arm, "Dear," Betty said kindly, "Is something on your mind?"

Martha collapsed the knitting needles in her lap and sighed. "It's Robert. I still haven't seen him. He missed school today. I'm worried."

Betty and the other women all sighed knowingly. "Teenagers are all the same, dear."

"My Anthony didn't speak to me for two years, you know. And now? We're the best of friends."

"It's hormones."

"He's probably got a girlfriend."

"He was just off with his friends."

"It's healthy for a boy his age to miss a few days of school."

"He probably slept through an alarm. Teenagers can never get enough sleep."

Martha supposed that any of these things could be true and she nodded, as if their statements were consoling.

On the walk home, Martha decided it was time to check on Robert. Just seeing him sleeping would comfort her. Luke scoffed and turned up the TV when she told him what she was doing.

There was a musty, vaguely dirty smell in the hallway outside

Robert's room. Martha opened the door a crack and peered in. The curtains of the window were hanging half-open and there was a stream of pale white-ish light coming in from the streetlight outside, illuminating the garbage on the floor. Shadowy in the light was a pizza box, a stack of plates, four video game controllers, a tangle of cords and socks, some dirty underwear, crumpled paper, the neck of a guitar, seven or eight Hotwheel cars, and a brownish-grey stain. In the bed, the vague outline of Martha's son could be seen, snoring gently in the middle of a heap of blankets. Martha sighed quietly, picked up the plates, untangled some of the socks, and backed out of the room without a word.

Robert hated when people went in his room. It was the only thing that he and Martha had ever argued about. Two years ago, Martha discovered that they were down to three forks and a champagne glass in the kitchen. When she went in search of her other dishes, she found the remainder of her forty-seven piece dining set piled in precarious, moldy heaps in one corner of her son's bedroom. When Robert came home to find his room tidied and amply febreeze-d, he flew into a rage and yelled at his mother for ten minutes. He was fuming for days but, after much raging, agreed to place dirty dishes outside the door or in the kitchen sink if he was to continue being allowed to eat in his room.

Since then, Martha had only entered Robert's room on Sunday's to vacuum and change the bed sheets, which she was permitted to do only while Robert was present. It had been many months since Martha was in the room, no vacuuming was done while Robert was absent, although dishes and clothes continued to appear outside the door periodically.

On Thursday, Martha called Steve's mother. Steve had been friends with Robert since the third grade and they were still close, although not nearly as close as they had been. Steve and Robert had little in common now, except their shared past, and only saw each other occasionally. Steve's mother was the only mother that Martha was in regular contact with. The other boy's mothers only called when the boys were staying the night, and only to confirm their child's whereabouts. They always sounded tired, slightly confused, and extremely suspicious. Jen, Steve's mother, always sounded pleasant.

"Oh, Martha," Steve's mother said.

"Jen. I was wondering if you'd seen Robert in the last few months."

"Oh? No, I don't think Steve-y's seen him in a good few months now. Though, we saw him at the supermarket in October, buyin' candy for you and Luke. Said hi, I think. Why's that Martha?"

"I was just wondering. He's been coming in late and leaving early and we haven't crossed paths."

"Oh, teenagers are like that, dear. Except Steve-y. He's always with his mom if he has the choice."

Steve's mother had seven boys. Steve, the youngest, was much coddled. This was one of the reasons Steve and Robert no longer had much in common.

"Hm."

"I'll let you know if we see him, though."

"Thanks, Jen."

"Oh, you betcha."

Martha was about to hang up the phone when she paused, "Jen?"

"Yeah?"

"What do you think I should do?"

Jen seemed to sigh, "Give him space, dear."

Martha thanked her, and hung up the phone.

She walked upstairs, opened Robert's door, and peered inside.

He was still asleep. Missing school. Two days in a row was odd. Robert loved school. He was a good student. She wondered if he was sick. She crept through the debris and placed a hand on his forehead; he seemed warm but not feverish. As Martha backed out of the room, careful not to step on anything important, Robert snored on.

The school called again, Martha let the call go to voicemail and headed to the tutoring center.

The children were awful. They kept picking their noses and flicking the boogers at one another. Every year, this habit evolved naturally in Martha's classroom. She couldn't tell where it began, who started it, or why it became so popular. The other teachers didn't have this problem. The thing would catch on at different times every year, but whenever it happened there was a good solid week of little to no productivity.

When Martha came home, she put potatoes on to boil, micro-waved a whole box of pizza pockets, and went upstairs. It didn't appear as though Robert had been out of bed. He was in the same position, curled up in a ball on top of a heap of blankets. She waved the pizza pockets in front of Robert's sleeping face. He gave no indication of consciousness. Usually, Robert could smell the freezer being opened downstairs, through the door of his bedroom.

She left the pizza pockets on the bedside table and backed out of the room.

On Saturday, the situation was much the same. No dishes or clothes were missing. The pizza pockets were untouched. She tried one. It was stale, tough and salty. She fed them to the cat and called Steve's mother again.

Jen sounded a little exasperated. "Martha, you should let the boy sleep. He probably has a girlfriend; he's spending all night out and sleeping it off during the day. He'll be back on his feet and back to school in no time."

On Sunday, Martha and Luke went to the state fair. They watched the horse show, pet some goats, and talked about work and politics. They rode the Gravitron and Luke threw up elephant ear all over her shoes. He was very sorry. He won her a goldfish at the milk-bottle booth. Martha missed Robert. On the way home they stopped at a taco place and ate dinner. The goldfish floated to the top of its bag and blinked at Martha in a terminal way.

When they got home, Luke turned on the TV and Martha walked into Robert's room. He was still asleep. No dishes had appeared. The cat had not touched the Pizza pockets.

On Monday, another call came from the school. Martha went into Robert's room and shook his shoulder. He didn't budge. She said his name very loudly, slapped his face gently, and kissed his ear. Robert hated ear kisses more than he hated people in his room. He didn't wake.

On Tuesday, Martha called the doctor. It took her a full twenty minutes to work up to the task. She called in sick at the tutoring center. They sounded annoyed. She called Luke. He was in a meeting. She called Steve's mother again, but she didn't answer. On Steve's mother's answering machine, Jen and Steve were singing a Christmas carol.

Martha shuddered.

Eventually, she called the doctor. The receptionist said he would be available for making house-calls from noon to four. At noon, the doorbell rang. The doctor was the same doctor who had delivered Robert. He was the only person that Martha trusted. When she was pregnant with Robert, she thought she was going to die. When she didn't die, she attributed this to the doctor. He was very, very old now, and the shape, color, and texture of an enormous walnut. He cleared his throat, which was like the sound of an ancient cannon firing. Martha flinched and welcomed him in.

The doctor measured Robert's heartbeat, muttered, "Oh my," looked inside his mouth and muttered, "Oh my, yes," peered inside both nostrils and one ear and said, "Oh yes, oh my," tickled the bottom of one enormous foot and said, "Oh yes." Martha stood quite still and quiet, not wanting to interrupt. The walnut doctor turned to her and nodded.

They sat down at the kitchen table. Martha put a Disney mug of instant coffee in front of the doctor.

"It seems Robert is hibernating," the doctor said. He took

a sip of coffee. When he put the mug back on the table's surface, Martha expected him to go on, but he did not.

"So… what do we do?"

The doctor shrugged, "Wait until spring."

Martha rubbed her temple. "Is there anything we can do…now?"

"Nope," the doctor said, "it's quite dangerous to wake them when they're like this."

"Should we take him to the hospital?"

"Dear me no, it's not contagious or life-threatening. He'll be fine May first."

"Is there anything you can…prescribe?"

"Not really. Rest, I guess."

"But, he's asleep."

The doctor nodded, "Oh, yes."

When the doctor left, Martha put on a Kate Bush album and turned the volume all the way up. The cat ran from the room. When Luke came home, he turned off the stereo and set a pizza box on the kitchen table. He sensed that something was amiss. Luke placed a piece of cheese pizza and a glass of wine in Martha's hand and sat down next to her on the couch without a word.

"Do you want to watch the game?"

Martha shrugged.

"What?" he asked, offering her another slice of pizza even though she hadn't touched the first.

"It's Robert," she said.

Luke rolled his eyes, "La-ti-da, what a surprise. Gah."

Martha took a large bite of pizza and through the hot cheese said, "The doctor says he's hibernating."

Luke turned on the TV and shrugged, "So?"

"Aren't you worried?"

"No. Why should I be? Bears hibernate, rabbits hibernate and stuff."

"But he's a boy."

Luke waved his hands around mockingly, "But he's a boy!"

Martha ate the rest of her pizza and went upstairs. She sat on the end of Robert's bed and stared at him for a little while. His beard had grown in. It was a fine, downy fuzz along his cheeks now, and his hair was getting long.

He was wearing the pajamas she had made him two Christmas's ago. She wondered if he had planned on hibernating, or if it just happened. She wondered if it was common for teenagers to hibernate.

On Wednesday night at knitting club, she told the ladies what the doctor had said. They looked confused. Some of them laughed.

"That can happen," said Betty, looking sympathetic. Martha unraveled her sweater, which looked more like a pair of pants anyway, and started work on a scarf.

The school stopped calling about Robert's absences. The kids in Martha's tutor class stopped flicking boogers. Luke bought her a new goldfish and put the bowl on her nightstand. On April thirtieth, Martha went into Robert's room. She had cleaned and vacuumed, changed the sheets beneath him by sliding his blanket ball onto the floor, and febreezed the room thoroughly. The freezer was stocked with pizza pockets and the refrigerator was stocked with soda. Martha had bought Robert new pencils, two new popular video games, and a glow-in-the-dark football. These gifts lay, wrapped in newspaper, at the end of Robert's bed in a tidy stack.

Luke came home with Chinese food, a Brad Pitt movie, and a large bag of potato chips. He microwaved the Chinese food while Martha went up to check on Robert.

"Give it a rest, Martha, he's not going anywhere," Luke said.

Robert's face was quite hairy now, and the hair on his head was long and stringy. His nose seemed longer, and he seemed much, much bigger. Martha was excited for him to wake up. She slept peacefully.

Luke shook Martha awake before her alarm. "I think

there's someone in the house, stay here, don't make a sound," he said hurriedly. He was dressed in a bathrobe and mismatched slippers. He held a crossbow in one hand and a baseball bat in the other. He sprinted out of the room.

She jumped out of bed and went to the top of the stairs. There was a snuffling, rummaging sound coming from the kitchen.

"Aha!" Luke yelled loudly, there was a loud, angry roar, the thwack of the crossbow burying itself in drywall, and slippered feet sliding on the wood floor. The front door slammed open on its hinges and there was another loud roar from outside. Unable to stand still any longer, Martha ran down the stairs and out the front door after Luke. He leveled the crossbow at the neighbor's back yard and let an arrow loose.

"Honey!" Martha called hoarsely, "Luke, stop!"

Luke turned around. "There was a god damn bear in the kitchen."

"What?"

"A bear. A forest creature, a bear. I didn't get it."

"Oh."

"Good thing too, I think they're endangered."

Martha peered through the darkness, then she remembered her son. "Robert!" she said, her eyes wide and she and Luke ran up to the bedroom.

Robert's room was empty, the newspaper-wrapped presents were still in a tidy stack, the ball of blankets was on the floor. She slid down the stairs, threw open the front door and plunged into the semi-darkness.

"Robert!" she yelled. A streetlight was blinking at the end of the street. A flashlight beam appeared behind her. Luke was at the other end of it.

They shone it around the houses and trees. Large indentations in the soft muddy ground cast huge black shadows in the light of the flashlight, "Damn bear."

Luke steered Martha back into the house. He sat her down

at the kitchen table and handed her a tumbler, into which he emptied a bottle of whiskey.

When Luke went outside to put a key under the mat, in case Robert came back, Martha stood up and opened the fridge. There were thirteen empty boxes of pizza pockets and a note: "More pizza pockets, please." Martha smiled.

IN ONE ROOM OF THE HOUSE

. • . • . .

In one room of the house someone masturbates on a drum set. Over the high hat, a little bit of ass crack is visible. When you open the door they don't turn, they just say, "It's okay, I know it's you, come in."

In another room of the house there is a person sleeping in a bed that you expect to be empty. The person makes room for you, even though you have only come into the room to get dressed for school. You grab your shoulder bag then drop it again. You slide into the covers and press your body against the body in your bed. Your faces are less than one inch apart and you fall asleep, the erection in your pants pressing against the warm, soft stomach of the person you did not expect to be in your bed.

In another room of the house, a person vomits into a toilet very quietly. You reach to hold their hair back for them. They are dressed in a wedding dress and their hair is a black wig. You pull the wig off of their head and they are not vomiting bent over the toilet, but facing you on their knees. They grab you by the ass cheeks and bury their face in your crotch.

In another room of the house a lot of birds fly around in

every direction. They keep hitting each other in midair and falling to the ground but for every pair of birds that fall, another pair takes flight. In the center of the room, someone moans sensually. When you try to beat the birds away to see who is in the center of the room, more birds take flight from the floor and push you back and it is then that you realize the floor is made of birds.

In another room of the house, there is someone playing guitar. They are playing a popular song but singing your name instead of the name in the lyrics. They are singing loudly. You cover your ears and cringe but they just sing louder.

So you close the door and walk into another room of the house. You can see out the window the second you walk in. There is a face outside the window. You know that every person you have encountered in the house is the same person. You feel like you should tell them you are taken, you are engaged, you are married, you are seeing someone, you are incapable of love, you are maybe obsessed, but you can't. You can't remember anything except the sweet breath, the soft stomach, the wedding dress, the loud singing, the pitter patter of ejaculate on the snare drum. You can't remember by whom you are taken, or why. You can't remember how it started or why you are continuing to open doors in the house. All you can remember is the face in your crotch. There is a soundtrack in the house that is a stumbling guitar rendition of a song you are familiar with. It's you playing the guitar, even though you don't play the guitar.

On the driveway outside the house the person from inside the house waits to be kissed. They stand; soft, white breasts exposed and pointed up in the chill night, their eyes closed. You slam the car door and sprint to them as fast as you can. While you reach for them, stumbling, they laugh and laugh.

In another room in the house, someone retches unsuccessfully in the bathtub. Their eyes are closed and when you enter they stop retching and start breathing deeply, heavily. Then they do not breathe at all. Ambulance sounds drift in the window from a little ways down the street. The phone rings and rings where it landed, on the tiles under the toilet, the window screen has a huge slit down the center. The bathroom smells like incense and menstrual blood.

In another room in the house, someone sits at a table by the window with a cup of coffee. Their hair is stringy and greasy, their face is pale, eyes sunken above dark, black circles. You sit down opposite them and feel easy, calm and happy when they start screaming at you, hitting everything in sight. Kicking out with more legs than you thought they possessed. They land a kick in the center of your back. You are immobilized. They are crying, but they seem more angry than sad.

On the driveway outside is an expanse of pale white sand. But when you reach to pick up a handful, it is packed hard, it is salt, not sand, and wind roars in your ears. There are mountains that you don't remember in the distance. This is not your driveway. But the half-naked person still stands there, waiting to be kissed. You consider walking to them but too much space separates you, it would take a day and a half to get there.

In another room of the house there is a bridge with a light in the very center. Everything else in the room is dark and blue, like a dense forest at night. You climb up onto the bridge from the side and you stand there, waiting for the person you know is there to appear from the dark edges.

In another room of the house is a corpse. It protrudes from behind a couch. Two bikes are leaning against the wall. Someone is sitting on the window ledge outside again, staring in longingly. But you don't open the window. And you don't look at the body. You sit down on the couch and wrap your sleeve around your nose and mouth. You turn on the television. Every channel is news. Every news report is about a shooting at the mall. A dozen people were killed, but all of the bodies are missing. You look behind the couch and survey the body.

In another room of the house, the person who was crying on the driveway is straddling another figure, the person's hips

117

are gyrating, pumping up and down on top of this other figure. You cannot see either person's face. You run to the person on top and grab their face, you grab their face in your hands and tear them up and away from the bottom person, who is still inside them as you kiss their face, bite their lip, drag them up off the ground, trying desperately to get their mouth on yours but everywhere you kiss is not a mouth.

In another room of the house you are watching the news report. They keep saying the same four lines, but someone is remixing the lines as they are said. "A dozen people dead today in a mall shooting downtown. The killer himself, shot by police outside the scene of the crime. A devastating event made more devastating by the disappearance of all twelve bodies from the scene moments later. If you have any information on the whereabouts of the bodies, please contact the station at once." "A dozen devastating events made more contact by the twelve station bodies. Devastating devastating disappearance of the station all at once. Killer mall shooting, killer outside. The killer outside, outside, outside, outside. Police shooting. Twelve moments to contact." "Stop," you say, the first words you have spoken in the house. "Stop, people are dying."

In another room of the house, the person you are with is packing up a suitcase. "I can't live like this. It's like you're haunting every room."

In another room of the house you find a person you didn't expect is curled up in your pajamas, sleeping peacefully in your twin bed. While they sleep you slide them out of the clothes they've stolen, you pull off their socks slowly, carefully. You untie the pajama bottoms and slip them over the person's shiny, sweaty thighs, down past their knees. You unbutton each small white button on the front of the soft, silk pajama shirt. You slide each small, soft arm out of each warm sleeve and you slide under the covers with the body. Your faces are so close you are breathing each other's exhaled breaths. And there are many exhaled breaths.

In the other rooms of the house, everything is quiet.

LAST CIGARETTE

· · · · ·

Anna moves through the crowded diner like a ballerina in a sea of flowers. Without looking, she fills a coffee cup up to the chipped ceramic brim. With a glance, she slices a pulled pork sandwich clean in half. She palms the register drawer shut and tears the white slip from its printer mouth in the same movement.

Anna hits the meal ticket wheel, snatches up four heaping plates the same as exhaling and with a twitch of the ruff on her pink apron, she whirls into the swinging counter door, nudging its rusty hinges outward with her hip. Onto the wet black and white tiles, spinning soundlessly, dropping each plate alongside corresponding cutlery and a napkin produced from nowhere onto the table of its respective owner. A nod, a careful smile, a gentle flourish in the napkin laying. Like a swan she slides into view of the last booth, where an occupant hails her with a wave of his index finger and before a word escapes his gravy-speck-led lips, Anna thrusts a bottle of ketchup into his outstretched palm.

Behind the counter, Anna stands like a Buddha when a family enters, shaking their umbrellas and stomping muddy rain boots in unison.

"Welcome, welcome, take a seat please," she says gruffly, sweeping a mop over the puddle they have created while one hand gathers the dirty plates and glasses off a nearby table, up into the crook of her arm and down to the waiting bus boy's anticipatory black plastic dish bin. All before the youngest child has even finished squeegeeing his raincoat onto the linoleum.

Anna resumes her counter vigil—deftly maneuvering a grilled cheese sandwich through a forest of flailing arms and onto the countertop, drawing out a coaster from a hidden apron pocket to place beneath a towering chocolate malt garnished, as her hands withdraw, by a bright red maraschino cherry.

A trickle of cherry juice begins its gelatinous journey down the mountain of whipped cream atop the malt as the cook rings the order bell with a hasty tap.

Anna nods to her relief shift, a pigtailed girl in a red cardigan and a triangular hat, as she unties the string of her pink-ruffed apron and ducks into the kitchen through a grey swinging door marred by a vertically rising sun of handprints in an ellipse across the left side.

***

Clumsily now, Anna fumbles with a bent-up Marlboro carton. Her hands tremble weakly as she sinks onto a vegetable crate in the kitchen-grease blackened alley. Doors slam and creak further down the alley as the other diner employees, laundry employees, and soup kitchen cooks cycle in and out of smoke breaks.

Anna's cigarette is sweat-damp, refuses to light. She flicks the pathetic plastic lever of her lighter: a dull, painful textured-metal scratching sound and nothing else.

Anna's face is a mountainside: grey-brown, pitted, sheer, but also formidable. Her eyes are wells—twin darknesses in a damaged visage. Her smile is a cave of confusion, a bent-up fissure in the weather-torn rock.

Her pale white lips purse around her damp cigarette, her body wracked by de-tensing tremors. Soon they will pass. Soon they will successfully shake out all of her crooked, seized-up muscles; shake them into complacent chords of proper impact-absorbing tissue.

Anna sighs a great, shuddering sigh and *click*, the lighter flame appears, a small blue nipple of light. She puffs her cigarette zealously, the paper tip crackles and simmers and her lungs expand with ghost-smoke.

She hasn't smoked for eleven years. No one has really smoked for eleven years. Only politicians and the devastatingly rich smoke cigarettes now. At first it was just another price hike. Then every tobacco plant in the world succumbed to blight, plunging the English-speaking world into another dark age.

Her body shivers as she imagines the ghost-smoke filling up her lungs. She drops the empty, glowing paper straw onto the grease-spattered concrete and grinds it to a pulpy white paste with the blocky bamboo heel of her shoe. Sometimes the action, the habit is enough. Her muscles are easily deceived.

"Anna," a voice says. It's the ketchup man from table seven. His hand stretches out in a greeting. Anna eyes him with skepticism, her hollow eyes reduced to fatal, stabbing slits, her tight white lips, an unyielding line.

The man is too well dressed in a long black jacket and rigid, square trousers the color of the deepest, purest puddle of kitchen grease. He has been stamped out of velvet fabric and pasted into the alley. He is a black gingerbread man lost in the pile of barely-breathing ectoplasm that is Anna's part of this city. His coat is wrinkled and there is a slight twitch in his blocky, muscular neck.

He handles the harpy glance of this diner woman with practiced grace. "I read your nametag, I didn't mean to startle you." His face is glacial. Slow, calm eyebrows freckle a thick, wide brow. Alien white skin the texture of cream, a dagger chin, white-blue eyes blink under the careless smattering of yellow eyebrows so sparse and thin they could be cobwebs.

Anna's murderous glare deepens. Somehow mistaking this for an invitation, he clears his throat and takes a step forward. Anna feels a fleeting twinge of youthful panic followed by instant scorn and self-reproach. As if, she quickly and bitterly remembers, she has anything to hide or protect.

"I'm sorry, I'm a little lost. I don't know my way around the—this part of town."

"The Slum, you mean," Anna interrupts. She hates when people don't say what they mean to say, hates it with the blind and unforgiving hatred of a person who themselves doesn't quite grasp why they should hate something.

But before she has begun to scold this man the color of marshmallow cream, he is simpering like a parent to an outraged infant, "My dear woman, I apologize if I have even remotely begun to offend. It was my very last wish…"

"What do you want," Anna interrupts again, spittle erupting in an angry cloud from her pursed lips and speckling the grease-puddle before her.

She hates wealthy people with a rage and conviction similar to her hatred of people who don't say what they mean. She has hated them for as long as she can remember, but not forever.

Anna, like all young girls, once yearned for wealth and power and comfort, when she believed that she could win it with what gifts are given to any sort of woman, regardless of her situation at birth. But those days of naïveté are gone. She prefers to live in squalor among the hordes of anonymous fiends who inhabit the slum, each dying from some putrescent illness derived of their absolute, woeful, and unforgivable poverty. Anna feels imperial and successful when she alone, standing straight-backed and sober in an ocean of the hunched and drunk. She feels massive, intimidating, fierce.

Marshmallow has taken another step. Anna's first venom-ous defense has failed her. She holds the icy gaze of the marsh-mallow man while peering around discreetly for a route of escape. He seems to smell this rabbity plotting and continues forward. With another step he will be at the kitchen door. All that remains is to flee down the filthy alley and slide into the next open door, the Chinese Laundry, or the soup kitchen.

"I merely noticed, as I was passing," Marshmallow offers, his baby-skin hands extended, pink palms upturned, "I thought that you might be looking for a smoke." One fresh pink hand flips a small white cylinder out of one sleeve in perfect conjunc-tion with his last word.

Anna stands slowly. Her bare knees creak and click like an old machine. The marshmallow man is a thick, even bar-rel shape: the same width at shoe level as the shoulder. He is a square and forbidding blockage at the end of the alley. And Anna is no fool. She knows that the chances of there being any tobacco at all in any cigarette within twenty miles of the slum are negligible. She knows that well-dressed, un-worked men with baby-hands and creamy skin are among the least trustwor-thy of all men, an untrustworthy gender to begin with.

Her blood gurgles faintly. From across the pavement she imagines that she can smell the tobacco leaf on the downwind as a breeze buffets their hair: Anna's grayish rat's nest piled into a lopsided bun behind a little triangular captain's hat; the marshmallow man's tight golden ringlets shivering on his pale scalp. The chances of this smell not being a pathetically hopeful hallucination, she knows, are nonexistent.

Anna grimaces defensively. Without a word the man pock-ets his almost-surely-fake cigarette and shrugs. His boulder shoulders turn and over one of them his voice carries, "I only needed a simple favor, Anna."

This recurring use of her name unsettles her. She is un-used to being addressed. Her own name sounds chalky and limp in the mouths of strangers. And all men and women are strangers to Anna. She has not heard her own name in a century, it seems. But then a surge of blood still rushing around her veins with imaginary nicotine flushes her craterous cheek. A simple favor, she reasons, in return for the first cigarette in eleven years and most likely the last of her life—no one would say that that was unreasonable.

A whole galaxy of memories unfolds before her eyes as she tentatively raises her hand to stop the marshmallow man from turning.

***

Anna is an unattractive fourteen-year-old at a girls' school in the country. Her classmates unanimously dislike her. Her limbs are gangly and thin, her body is oddly full-figured, and the combination of her high forehead, thin hair, and craterous acne create a frightful head. She eats her lunches alone. She goes to the restroom alone. She does not whisper little secrets and dares to anyone after the lights are turned out and the matron is snoring in her chambers. She does not take part in the general foolish behavior of the other girls: she does not puncture hot water bottles in her classmate's beds, she does not set traps for little animals and set them loose in teachers' offices, she does not switch the other girl's uniforms so that one or the other of them thinks they are rapidly getting fatter or skinnier. She has never put salt in anyone's grape juice. She has never blown a spit wad at the back of anyone's head. She has never been in a three-legged race. She has never played truth or dare.

Anna sits on the founder's rock by herself and reads a book. She does not like books, really. She does not like reading. But both books and reading are better than thinking about how you are alone.

A fat girl with round, red cheeks and blue eyes sits on an adjacent rock and begins to cry loudly. It is an impressive performance. One moment she is crying, bawling, the next she is sitting perfectly still, her lip quivering gently as she contemplates her shoelaces. Then a burst of watery sobs. Then silence. Sobs. Silence. Sobs.

"What on earth are you doing that for," Anna asks not, of course, meaning to sound unkind. The fat girl's sobs, silenced as she listened to Anna speak, burst forth with renewed strength.

"They…they…they," she blubbers, "they hit me and pulled my ha…ha…ha…hair." She draws out this last syllable into a full seven-second cry, during which Anna's face screws into an expression of disgust.

"Why didn't you hit them back?" Anna asks, the loathing and repulsion clear on her pink, pitted face.

The blubberer stops. She sucks in her lip with what appears to be a great effort and looks at Anna curiously. "Oh," she says simply, as if this hadn't occurred to her.

Placing her index finger in her book to hold the page, Anna jumps down from her rock and slides up onto the fat girl's rock. She feels electric, like a charged wire about to be applied to a battery. She feels renewed.

"Hey," the fat girl says, wiping her large cheeks on the sleeve of her uniform, "do you, do you want a cigarette?"

Anna nods and slowly, bravely, she takes her finger out of her book and closes it on the rock beside them. The fat girl digs around in her bra for a while, jostling the multiple pink folds of her neck and bosom and finally extracts a small brown carton of cigarettes. "My sister sends them to me," the fat girl says, "she lives in New York, she's a model."

The fat girl chuckles good-naturedly at the look on Anna's face. "She's my half-sister, on my dad's side."

With a gentle pat, the fat girl pops one cigarette up out of the carton and puts her mouth around the end. She slides the cylinder out of the pack and extends it to Anna.

Anna gives it a pat, but nothing happens. She digs around in the small hole at the top and pinches the end of a filter. She slides the cigarette out of the carton and puts the filter end between her lips. The girl draws out a small, golden lighter. "I keep this right in the crack. No one's spotted it yet."

Anna tries not to panic as the heavy, sticky, woody smell of the cigarette clouds up her nostrils and lungs. The fat girl lights the tiny lighter, lights her own cigarette, then Anna's. The smoke curls up and stings her eyes.

"You have to inhale, dummy, like this," she breathes in deep and the end of her cigarette crackles. "Haven't you smoked before?" Anna breathes in and coughs desperately, the cigarette goes out.

***

"A favor?" Anna snaps, her fist raised up in front of her like a weapon. The marshmallow man steps close enough so that it is now impossible to imagine that the smooth, earthy scent he is emanating is a hallucination.

"A quick little task and you'll be on your way. Really, I just need an opinion, another..." he smiles, extending his hand again. In the palm is a perfectly cylindrical, unfiltered, hand-rolled cigarette. The brown bark, the texture, the smell, the sweet, thin aroma. It is bursting with genuine tobacco. "Perspective."

***

They step from the alley into a beam of grayish sunlight. Light loses most of its power on the journey down through the smog, more as it bounces off windows, stone gargoyles and heavy, absorbent brick. There is a clean black car parked in front of the wide diner window. The windows of the car are tinted black. A faint silhouette is visible through the tinted glass—the backseat of the car, or a woman's elbow. Anna is unsure. She is shuffled up against the car, her pink ruffed apron touching the cold, wet metal before the door beneath her opens a crack and she is whispered into the interior like water disappearing down a fissure in a rock.

The interior of the car is dark, but the oddly colored light bulbs on the diner's front awning are still visible and behind the smudged glass is Anna's relief shift—a young girl with pigtails wearing a red cardigan and a triangular captain's hat. The girl's eyes are glossy and wide. She stands perfectly still as the car purrs loudly and skids off into the street. Anna looks out the back window, following the girl with her eyes, watching her little hands wring the end of the mop handle like she has seen something distressing. The lights of a police car round the corner and everything is suddenly multi-colored, then too far away to see.

Anna shifts back into her seat and peers into the darkness beside her. There is indeed a body there, although all features are indistinguishable. She scrutinizes the shadow for a moment before the figure shifts and a little pillar of flame bursts out of the dark. A curiously greenish face and a moist-looking hand appear around the flame, then disappear as the end of a cigarette smolders, and the main source of light is extinguished. The green-gray lips remain visible, and the rounded tip of a fat, low nose as the smoker inhales, turns, and puffs a cloud of heavily perfumed smoke into Anna's scowling face. She breathes deeply, inhaling the half-used smoke with some foul herb scent. The cab of the vehicle fills with the smell of tobacco smoke and, lazily, She half-closes her eyes.

Anna was not addicted to cigarettes, not really. Not like some others. Anna quit after the first wave of blight ravaged the plants on the continent. One pack of cigarettes quite suddenly cost Anna an entire day's wages. Others, as poor or poorer than she, still lined up at the liquor stores Fridays and Mondays when the shipments came in, handing over a day's, or for some a week's wages for a single pack. For months Anna shivered and shook whenever she passed a smoker in the street, her blood urged her forward, urged her toward them to smell them, to ask them. But she knew she was more likely to receive a kick in the ribs than a regretful rejection, and she never asked. Not once.

When cigarettes went completely out of style, and then completely off the market, Anna stopped shivering altogether.

Anna examines the form. It seems feminine in its movements, the smooth wetness of its visible skin. But it is most definitely masculine, gargantuan, in size. Fear has not yet entered her. She feels alert, defensive, but not afraid. Until the creature speaks.

"Anna," the wet, green lips say slowly. "Annnnnnnnna."

***

When Anna's parents die, they leave her nothing but their massive debt and a store-bought card for her seventeenth birthday, signed and dated four months in advance. Anna leaves the girl's school and moves into a small flat that is wet with the smell of cat piss and mold.

At seventeen, Anna's looks have not improved, but her once soft, dazed expression has been eternally soured by the cruelty of others. Walking back to the flat with a bag of groceries, a tall, blond young man, seeing her struggle with the damp paper bag, offers to take her to her door. She scrutinizes the man with pursed, white lips. Deeming him less suspicious than anyone might expect, Anna hands him the groceries and, straightening her skirt, she sniffs heartily. They walk in silence. The man is tall, straight-backed and smartly, but cheaply dressed.

They stop at her door. "You live here?" the man says conversationally, one small black eye darting from the key in Anna's hand to the chipped cement stair, to her pointed nose, to the groceries in his arms like a fly at a bake sale. The other eye stays pointed vaguely in her direction, unfocused and eerily cloudy. Anna inhales through her teeth.

The man slowly turns his face so that the still eye is invisible, proffers the groceries and turns to descend the stairs.

Pity and horror rise in Anna. She did not see the eye when he approached her. It is such a terrible marring. He has a handsome face, she thinks, without it. "Coffee?" she calls awkwardly, like a bark or a goose honk.

He turns, once more showing only the good half of his face. "Coffee? Yes," he says graciously, bowing slightly.

When they make love, he forces her to look into the eye, to peer into its icy, sightless depths. He holds her neck and closes the good eye as he comes. The bad eye remains wide-open, unmoving, glassy, and cool.

Afterward, his bad eye trained upon the wall, the man shares his cigarette with Anna. She inhales as deeply as she can, she draws the ember down a whole quarter inch and puffs the smoke out like a backfiring car, with a rasping cough.

"You are an ugly thing aren't you," the man says, his good eye trained on her, appraising.

***

Minutes pass and Anna's back and neck grow stiff. She is not used to being still and she is trying very hard not to move. She remembers her relief shift. The red cardigan. She wonders if Red Cardigan called the police. She wonders if Red Cardigan remembers her name. Anna tries to remember Red Cardigan's name and comes up with nothing. There is a void where the recollection of an introduction would have been. There is no name. Anna, too, has no name. But there are others that will miss her, wonder where she has gone, come and find her. She carefully formulates a sentence along these lines, a sentence to say to the faceless green creature seething in smoke beside her as the car bumps down an unfamiliar street.

But all she can muster is a quick, rheumatic cough.

A deep, sonorous chuckle boils up from the seat bottom, slightly higher than the dull rumble of the engine.

"Don't worry, Anna, you're safe now."

Anna thinks about the cigarette in marshmallow man's palm. Is he driving now? She cannot see the windshield or the driver. Would she have been able to snatch the cigarette from his palm before he closed it? Maybe, though she was never quick at anything. Would he have given it to her if she asked? Would she have asked? She should have bargained better. She should have taken the last smoke first.

And she feels lonely. For the first time in decades, Anna feels alone.

***

In the night, the fat girl comes to her bedside and says, "I'm too afraid to go to the showers by myself, please come with me," Anna crawls out of the covers and puts her feet in her slippers on the splintery wood floor.

"Are we allowed?" She mouths.

"I can't take showers with the other girls, please come with me."

They share a cigarette by the bathroom window and the fat girl says, "Shower with me, come on."

In the steam from the faucets, the fat girl suddenly disappears and Anna is alone in the bathroom. Her hand shaking, she switches off the faucet. She feels around for her towel and clothes on the wooden bench where she left them, but there's nothing there.

***

Anna's heart pounds. "My," she stutters, "my cigarette." Her lips feel cold.

"Of course, dear," the green lips smack wetly, "your cigarette."

THE PAPER NAUTILUS

•᛫᛫᛫᛫•᛫᛫

Alastor van Devere wears corduroy underwear every day. He has thirty-nine pairs so he only has to do laundry every thirty-eight days. Sometimes it seems like even longer than thirty-eight days because there are some days that Alastor van Devere wears the same pair of corduroy underwear as the day before. Sometimes when he senses danger, Alastor van Devere wears two pair of corduroy underwear at once.

I wear a blue elephant mask every day. It has a long rubber nose and two small eyeholes. I wear this blue elephant mask because I have no face.

We live most of the year in a green sea turtle. The sea turtle is more spacious than it looks from the outside. Alastor van Devere, in his corduroy underwear, and I in my blue elephant mask, have all the comforts that modern humans need and expect from their homes and communities. This includes public parks, bicycle lanes on major roads, frozen microwave dinners, a big red sofa, and three pet mice named Albert, Susan, and Genoa.

There are many other happy couples living in sea turtles nearby, and many live aboard the Paper Nautilus. We travel slowly in a defensive formation. We travel at least four leagues per day.

***

Heavy metal can be a form of black magic, when there are naked dancers dancing in a clearing in the forest at 3:00 am. Heavy metal is a form of black magic and a built-in feature of Alastor van Devere's corduroy underwear.

There is a tall thin man with a dream-catcher for a head who visits the clearing where Alcest is danced to at 3:00 am. His fingers are branches of an olive tree and have the unique ability to rearrange the stars.

When the man with a dream-catcher head rearranges major constellations to confuse lonely sailors, it is usually the Paper Nautilus that seeks them out and delivers them to their destination.

The Paper Nautilus has some features that distinguish it from former Nautilus's. The first is its size and complex network of well-maintained highways over and through its several large urban areas.

A former captain of the Paper Nautilus once re-wrote the story of Snow White with many incestuous, pedophilic, lesbionic undertones. The re-telling of this classic children's tale was widely celebrated aboard the Paper Nautilus but had only limited success elsewhere.

Another distinguishing feature of the Paper Nautilus is its thin, semi-conscious symbiotic external membrane. This membrane, which scholars aboard the Paper Nautilus have long studied and speculated about, seems to have been a feral membrane descended from the abandoned membranes of other Nautilus's several generations ago. The Nautilus's re-domestication of this membrane makes it unique among Nautilus's.

***

On the deck of the sea turtle awash with dawn light, sun barely risen over the steep-making spires and plunging causeways of a city on the shore in the distance, several leagues out from the fleet, Alastor van Devere is in his corduroy underwear and I am in my blue elephant mask. We are drinking morning tea and preparing to watch the daily flagellation of the Paper Nautilus as it rises from beneath the surface. Overcome with ecstasy that another sun has risen over another city four leagues out from the fleet, it leaps twirling into the air, tentacles awhirl, slapping the surface of its semi-conscious symbiotic external membrane, enormous blue eyes sparkling with joy. The Paper Nautilus, so easily overcome and in a perpetually positive mood, child-wonder coursing through its re-domesticated external membrane, is the second to last living Nautilus in the ocean. It doesn't understand, the scholars hypothesize, the nature of its existence, nor the gravity of its penultimate status among Nautilus's, nor the impending extinction of its species.

***

It has been hard to ride the train from the sea turtle to the city every day, Alastor van Devere, I am happy we are moving into your brother's old flat above the pipe shop next week. I know his bodily fluids are all over it, but I don't think it's anything a little tiger urine and some Vaseline won't fix.

***

According to "The Society for the Transference of the Title 'Pterology' from the Study of Ferns to the Study of Underground Pterodactyls," the last known pterodactyl was killed by friendly fire in 1934. It has been almost a hundred years since the last pterodactyl was sighted, but evidence of their continued presence among us still manifests periodically, indicating that the noble race has simply withdrawn from what it would inevitably find to be an unfriendly, unforgiving modern world.

In Southern Turkey, a young man by the name of Ahkbar reportedly lost seven to eight teeth in the middle of the night. There was no apparent cause. It was a great trouble for local authorities who were accused of neglecting their duties as protectors of the peace, but members of "The Society for the Transference of the Title 'Pterology' from the Study of Ferns to the Study of Underground Pterodactyls" at once recognized the true nature of the event to be an indication of the presence of a Pterodactyl.

***

Dear Alastor van Devere,

I think we're both better off alone now, at least for a while. We told each other we would see where this led us and I think it's becoming increasingly clear that we aren't right for each other, not, at least, in THAT sense.

I left a pair of corduroy underwear in the back seat of your hatchback; I stuck them through a gap in the back window. You left them on my doorstep the other night.

***

The platform of "The Society for the Transference of the Term 'Pterology' from the Study of Ferns to the Study of Underground Pterodactyls" is considered valid by only a small portion of the scientific community. The platform states that the primary cause of the grievous lack of interest in, and scholarship, concerning the Pterodactyl is that there is no suitable term in the English language to describe the particular field of study. Their short-term goals are spreading Xeroxed copies of pamphlets around public restrooms in coastal towns. Their long-term goal is the legal acquisition of the term "Pterology."

***

Alastor van Devere wears corduroy underwear because he likes the feel of the corduroy against his genitals – and corduroy is a durable, largely stain-resistant fabric. He has been wearing corduroy underwear for eleven years – since he lost seven to eight of his front teeth to what some scholars believe to have been a Pterodactyl in the middle of the night.

***

1. Pterodactyls are predisposed to practice amateur dental surgery.

2. Pterodactyls are kleptomaniacs.

3. Pterodactyls don't have any teeth.

These three facts have been shown to lead to an increase in the belief that black magic (heavy metal) is responsible for the nighttime loss of seven to eight front teeth.

Pterodactyls don't have any teeth, which means that they cannot get cavities, and so they eat a lot of sweets and never have to think about the repercussions.

***

I wear the blue elephant mask because I do not have a face.

***

The man with a dream-catcher for a head who sometimes dances in black magic (heavy metal) rituals has golden teeth sewn into his dream-catcher that he gnashes when aroused.

When Alastor van Devere and I are watching the heavy metal (black magic) rituals from the deck of our semi-spacious sea turtle four to five leagues from shore and the crest of the sea turtle is glimmering with starlight, Alastor van Devere pulls on an extra pair of corduroy underwear.

***

Sometimes I feel unprotected and exposed when the fleet of sea turtles is waiting for the Paper Nautilus to return with provisions, directions, and a couple of lonely sailors.

***

In the city a woman is shopping. No one told the woman that all of her children were bringing friends home from school with them. There are only two cans of tuna in the pantry. So the woman is shopping. The woman is shopping for fifty-six teenagers. The woman hates all of her children. She thinks she might have expected that they would stay cooing, mewling infants eternally. The woman should not have had twenty-eight children. The woman is shopping for ingredients for a meat-less, cheese-less, gluten-free lasagna for fifty-six teenagers with diverse dietary restrictions. The steep-making spires and the plunging causeways of the city are visible through the stained glass roof of the supermarket where the woman is shopping and thinking about how much she hates her twenty-eight children, and their twenty-eight friends, because no one told her that all of her twenty-eight children were bringing friends home from school to stay for dinner.

***

Back on the Paper Nautilus, lions with no manes are prowling the rainforest through which a huge, well-maintained six-lane highway stretches. The tentacles of the Paper Nautilus are splashing the ocean and it is swooping and diving through tall waves like a big, spectacular bird. On board the Paper Nautilus, the members of "The Society for the Transference of the Title 'Pterology' from the Study of Ferns to the Study of Underground Pterodactyls" is growing sea-sick as they pack Napalm bombs to exterminate the forest and rid the Paper Nautilus of ferns forever.

***

A lonely sailor rescued by the Paper Nautilus is sitting on the edge of the highway that stretches from one edge of the Paper Nautilus to the other. It is the largest highway on the Paper Nautilus, and the busiest. The lonely sailor is watching and waiting for the ocean to give him a sign that he is supposed to be aboard the Paper Nautilus, a sign that the hollowness in his heart will fade, or that the ocean would not welcome him if he plummeted into it from the highway, but would spit him back up, or that his death would stop something huge from moving – a sign from the ocean that his death would be like a spoon in a garbage disposal. He is waiting for someone on the highway to stop him, or someone on the Paper Nautilus to notice that he is gone. The lonely sailor feels like the Paper Nautilus. He feels like the second to last lonely sailor left in the ocean. All of his friends and his family were killed or eaten by sea beasts when their boat ran ashore because someone had rearranged the stars. He feels like the second to last lonely sailor in the entire ocean.

It has been a long time and the ocean is not doing anything (or, at least, from his height it is not doing anything), Were he closer to the ocean, he would see that it is frowning at him and mouthing angrily, "I will spit you back out!". So the sailor touches his cold cheeks one last time, rubs his fingers together lovingly, smiles one last bright, radiant smile and, laughing to himself, he dives over the edge of the Paper Nautilus. Down, down, down, the lonely sailor falls for so long that he seems to be hovering static in resistant liquid before with a mighty splattering sound the lonely sailor lands in a field of sticky blue mucus. He tries to move but his body is stuck to the surface of the field by the thick, gluey fluid. The lonely sailor pries his face off of the field which, under the mucus-y layer, is slick and glass-like and looks around him.

He seems to be on the top of a shallow blue hill.

The lonely sailor tries to push himself up but he is stuck like a fly to flypaper.

The hill of sailorpaper seems to shift, he feels himself move with it. Then there is a low moaning sound that comes from deep within the hill, or far, far below it.

The lonely sailor realizes with a great shock that he has landed on the eyeball of the Paper Nautilus.

The Paper Nautilus moans again. The lonely sailor can only interpret this sound as a sound of annoyance. He does not speak the language of the Paper Nautilus.

"I'm sorry, Oh I'm so sorry," says the lonely sailor, beginning to cry, "I didn't mean to land here, I didn't mean to hurt anyone, I hope you're not hurt. Look at me, I can't even kill myself right."

The Paper Nautilus moans again, somewhat sympathetically, the lonely sailor thinks.

***

When the Paper Nautilus leaves the fleet to rescue lonely sailors, our sea turtle always quivers with unease. There are many ravenous sea beasts that would like to capture our sea turtles and drag them up onto the cliffs of the California coast and fry them in the sun for eating later. The sea beasts that want to cook and eat our sea-turtle are captained by appointed government officials. There are no free elections aboard the ravenous sea beasts.

***

"I want to die because I am the last sailor in the ocean," the lonely sailor confides to the eye of the Paper Nautilus. "It feels like there isn't any point because no matter how hard I look, I'll never find another sailor in the ocean. I'll be alone forever. I can't go on knowing I'll be alone forever."

There is a long silence, the lonely sailor can feel the Paper Nautilus breathing evenly beneath him, he can see the pupil of the Paper Nautilus' eye a few yards away. And then suddenly the mucus-y sailor-catching layer of eye fluid begins to thin, he is sliding down the face of the eye. The Paper Nautilus is crying.

"I'm sorry," the sailor cries, grasping at the smooth glasslike surface over which he is now sliding with his finger nails, hoping he is not hurting the Paper Nautilus even more. "I didn't mean to make you cry. I just don't know how YOU do it – how you go on so cheerfully, every day, knowing that you are the second to last Paper Nautilus in the ocean – that one day you will probably be the last."

The Paper Nautilus begins to moan again, but this time it is not a sympathetic sound. It is a sound of untranslatable, unquantifiable despair.

The lonely sailor slides in a waterfall of tears, over the lid of the eye of the Paper Nautilus and into the disapproving ocean.

***

Alastor van Devere seems unusually sad this morning. His corduroy underwear is chaffing. His eyes are red and swollen with sleeplessness. He has been up all night soothing the sea turtle, listening for the sound of the Paper Nautilus' return. We drink our tea in a bitter silence.

***

The sea turtles miss the Paper Nautilus, they are calling to one another. They are worried.

***

Someone has explained to the Paper Nautilus that it is the second to last Nautilus in the ocean. All other Nautilus's have grown ten-toed feet and crawled up the cliffs of the California coast to live peaceful, half-conscious lives in the city of steep-making spires and plunging, narrow causeways.

The network of well-maintained highways running over the surface of the Paper Nautilus is empty. The membrane has taken flight. Sun-burned lions with no manes roam the desolate stretches of pavement between the major cities of the Paper Nautilus scavenging, eating the remains of cactus plants – the only plants left alive aboard the Paper Nautilus.

***

Inside the elephant mask I make a sobbing noise and Alastor van Devere or the sea turtle, or one of the three mice, or some combination of them, kiss the palms of my outstretched hands and the end of the rubber nose of the elephant mask.

***

The Paper Nautilus returned today, but all of the cities and highways were empty.

Lions with no manes and Pterodactyls with necklaces of human teeth prowled the empty pavement and circled ominously above the cities and towers aboard the Paper Nautilus. "The Society for the Transference of the Title 'Pterology' from the Study of Ferns to the Study of Underground Pterodactyls" released seventy-four hand-assembled napalm bombs over the rainforest of the Paper Nautilus, destroying every last fern and winning the court case to determine if the

142

title "Pterology" should be transferred from the study of ferns to the study of Pterodactyls.

Pterodactyls returned in full force to the cities of the Paper Nautilus with their dental surgery equipment and their big, toothless beaks gnashing.

There was never any such thing as a pterodactyl in most of the cities and towns aboard the Paper Nautilus, and no one had an emergency escape plan.

All were killed.

***

A woman in the city doing her shopping watches through the stained glass ceiling of the supermarket as a flock of pterodactyls fly overhead. Great sea-turtles were dragged up on the cliffs of the California coast to fry in the sun and Alastor van Devere, in his corduroy underwear and I in my blue elephant mask, settled in for the ride as our sea turtle bucked and kicked, fighting with all of its might against the sea beasts dragging it to shore.

THE LION TAMER

In waking there is fear. The waking fear is fear of finding the door open and lions in the room. Samuel does not have this fear. The door may be made of particleboard and dust, but it is locked securely by fourteen locks and one Chinese finger trap.

I cough discreetly. Samuel's sleep-scowl deepens. All around us the walls shake plaster dandruff down on everything we own: a stack of daily papers, a dirty cup and saucer, half a sandwich and a silk hat box.

Plaster dandruff snows on us in bed. Sheets are crumpled under us. It is hot and dusty in our ash-white compartment.

With the careful slowness of a fairly confident affection, I peel my arms away from his arms and slide down from the small bed and onto the floor, where tiny whirls of plaster dust rise around me, wrapping me in their tendrils. My nose itches. Samuel's sleep-scowl has risen into sleep-surprise. He is dreaming about breakfast, his lips twitch anxiously. I see soft plaster dust falling on the orange-y plane of his cheek, dangling from the high-wire of his eyelashes.

I scoot across the snowy floorboards to the sandwich. I blow some of the dust off and take a pensive bite.

145

The compartment shivers and jolts sharply as the huffing engine drives the wheels across another rail. If there are wheels. Or any other rails. If there is an engine.

Samuel has been on top of the dining car, he told me when we met. He has seen the animals that drive us and they are not, as are supposed, loud fire-breathing metal creatures but soft, grey, large-eared and slow. Our speed is an illusion. Our movement is not perpetual. No one is awake all of the time. It is impossible to know if the train stops for an hour while you sleep to trade one weary elephant for a fresh one at intermittent check-points.

I am skeptical of this theory. I am skeptical of all theories.

***

In the dining car an old man with a beard is playing chess with a bear. The bear is a retired circus bear. He is as old and withered as the old man with the beard. The bear's beard is as grey and tangled as the old man's. The bear's fur is patchy and thin. He is hunched over so far that his snout protrudes from his stomach. His spine is the shape and color of a rainbow, arching from the back of the seat to the base of his gnarled, patchy neck. He is wearing a blue ruff and faded striped clown suit. Only one red pom-pom remains on the front of the suit. It is like a big red bellybutton. The bear makes a move and grumbles "Check."

The old man strokes his yellow grey beard and licks his lips. He seems to taste a little bit of food in one corner. The grey-pink eel nose of his tongue flicks out and slaps against this corner for a while.

The old man moves his king. It is his last piece. The bear moves his pawn. It is his last piece. "Check," the bear says.

I sit down across the aisle from them and ask the waiter for a bowl of salt and a spoon. I never drink coffee alone. The taste of coffee when you are in company is the taste of a quiet room full of sleeping people where you are the only person awake. The taste of coffee when you are alone is the taste of being the last person on a train, the taste of infinite sadness.

The waiter brings the salt and I spoon it onto the boomer-ang-patterned Formica surface of the table. With the spoon I spread the salt out evenly across the table. I draw a sandwich and sit back to watch the shaking of the compartment erase the table drawing by shifting the salt back into an even sheet.

The dining car of this train does not shake as much as our compartment, which we built ourselves from other, abandoned compartments. This is the reason our compartment shakes. It was too difficult to detach and reattach the huge and stubborn metal coils that elevate compartments like the dining compartment, making them jostle gently on the rails as they trundle along, instead of shivering like injured horses. I feel mysterious. The bear and the old man are still playing chess. They are not playing by the rules. But they are playing by some rules. Or maybe they are not playing at all, just passing time.

"I thought of something," the old man says to the bear.

"Oh?" The bear says rhetorically, shifting his pawn toward the old man's king.

"I thought about that bicycle you used to ride."

The waiter approaches the two and whispers something in the bear's ear. The bear grunts uncomfortably as he wrenches himself with considerable difficulty from the seat. He jostles the table in his attempts to rise and the old man's king topples. "Check mate," the old man says, rising as far as he can manage out of his seat to shake the bear's tremendous, clawed paw. "Good game."

The bear grunts and as he turns to shamble down the narrow aisle of the dining car to the wall-mounted plastic telephone in the adjacent car, one of his black claws rakes the wrist of the old man. A thick river of blood appears on the old man's arm. It begins to trickle down onto the table and the chess game.

The old man seems confused. The bear and the waiter have reached the end of the car and are preparing to duck into the next car. The old man seems as if he wants to cry out. In his confusion he waggles his bleeding arm around and splatters blood all over the dining car.

I lose my appetite and take a huge, deep breath. I exhale, blowing the sheet of salt into the air where it hovers lazily for a moment, then drops, tinkling off of silverware and other Formica tabletops. It lands in the bearded man's blood and on his yellow white beard.

Waiters are rushing toward the old man now. They are wrapping up his wound and carrying him down the aisle. I look around the bloodied table. I look under the table and on the seats and under the seats and under the table. There are no other chess pieces.

***

Bloody footprints follow me like little animals as I make my way down the cars to the car where our compartment is nestled snuggly between two other compartments. The compartment on the left is dark and sounds of sleepiness are inside it. The compartment on the right is light and sounds of glass breaking again and again come from it.

The passage is dark. At the end of the passage, eyes are looking up toward me. They are so close to the floor that the owner of them must be lying down. The eyes are huge and I know it is a lion at once. My hands are sweating. I fumble with the clasp on the door to our compartment. I slam the door behind me and sink to the floor, my heart racing.

Samuel has already woken and is lying in the plaster dust on the floor. It is drifting in and out of his nostrils. The thing about the plaster dust is that Samuel and the plaster dust get along very well. He takes care of it and it is kind to him. But the plaster dust and I are not on good terms. We have a lot of communication problems. He breathes in and out and jealousy stabs me. The jealousy is also hunger, or accompanied by hunger. It is hard to say. The one bite of dusty sandwich in my stomach is rolling over and over. I can feel that it is lonely. I would be less hungry with a more empty stomach.

I lie down beside him in the dust and tell him this.

I will lie in the dust when he is in the dust, but I seldom drop down this low in our compartment unless I am with him. I follow him many unpleasant places.

Today, he says, we are going to purchase a cactus.

***

On the train, there are many cacti. The cactus is the most common plant native to the train. There are ancient, brittle cacti and young, limey green cacti. All cacti are edible. All cacti are for sale. Some cacti have overbearing personalities. Some cacti are very shy, others grow out of the woodwork of door jams and exist for the express purpose of snagging sweaters. Some cacti are kept in pots and others have decorative foliage in their pots, which obscures them from view and replicates their natural habitat. This makes them more comfortable. When a cactus is comfortable, you are more likely to observe its natural behaviors. Some cacti have strict diets. Some have exotic colors. Some cacti have been seen migrating across ceilings and along the molding of the floors. Cacti can be painful to step on. Some cacti are poisonous. Some have special healing properties. Some have special hallucinogenic properties. Choosing a cactus with hallucinogenic properties is not forbidden, but it is not recommended.

Samuel spends many hours examining the spines and ridges of the cacti. As he is examining the many aspects of the cacti that must be considered before purchasing one, Samuel mutters about the ideal circumstances under which we would purchase a cactus. It would have four prongs, potentially five.

It would be small, round, and buxom. We would feel connected to it, emotionally, at first sight. Samuel sighs and shakes his head. His back is arched in a way that shows two mountains where his shoulders are, and a great wall where his spine is. One side of his back is China. The other is Mongolia. A figure leads a host of Huns. It is an iconoclast. It is a battlefield soaked in blood.

I slouch forward over the battlefield, my small breasts smashing into the Huns. The Chinese rejoice. The wall crumbles with age.

"Really, I don't believe it is too much to ask to find a cactus with a wooly turtle complexion."

This is how Samuel has been describing the color of the cactus that we should purchase if the ideal circumstances were to arise. "Wooly turtle." I cannot picture Wooly Turtle as a color. I can only picture a turtle in a sweater. This, to me, is just as good. China is entering an age of enlightenment when Samuel stands upright, gently shoving me off. Chinamen and the corpses of the Huns tumble off the vertical plane, landing with inaudible thumps on the floorboards of the car.

We return to the dusty compartment cactus-less. Samuel is disappointed. I am nervous. When we open the door to our compartment, there is a large dusty form. "It is the lion," I whisper, recognizing the peculiar shape of a sleeping lion beneath the plaster dust.

"It is the hat box," Samuel responds. He walks forward. My heart beats up into my throat and I clutch it, trying to force it back down. Samuel shakes the dust off of the hatbox and hands it to me. "See?"

"Our compartment has a lot of dust," I say.

Samuel pats the dust on the wall. It curls around his fingers and swirls up his arm, giving him a brief hello-hug before it flutters down to the creaky floorboards.

***

I dream that we have a child together and it is a baby turtle. We hold her soft, wrinkled body between us. She is named Ioletta, our fathers named her and decorated her room with small white roses. We love her with all our hearts. But there has been a mistake.

Ioletta is not our child. We never had a child. That is when I wake.

Samuel snores comfortably on the couch. I am curled in a tight ball on our bed, my body clenched in dream sadness.

***

I watch out the window of the hospital car. Many people lie in beds around me. I am sitting in a chair. An old man with his head propped up on a suitcase instead of a pillow sings loudly, otherwise it is quiet. I am sterilizing surgical instruments which include a tiny hammer, a bone saw covered in crusted gore and dry cracking blood, and many long, rusted needles. The doctors in the hospital car are not trustworthy. Their methods are extreme and often overzealous. Yesterday they castrated a man for premature baldness. The doctors are great supporters of Eugenics. There are mandatory sterilization policies for many illnesses, including stuttering and gingivitis.

The window is flashing bright and then dark and then bright and then dark from the swaying light in the center of the car. The singing man is singing a song about whales. Sometimes he gets very quiet and just hums. This is when the whales fall in love. It is something that no one can vocalize, not even Pognafio, which is the name of the singing man. He has been in the hospital car for many years. The doctors have been treating him, slowly but surely, for stage fright. Their methods, as always, are questionable but at least in this case, seem to be effective.

When the circus car was still visited by many people, Pognafio was a great opera singer. One day the baboons escaped from the circus car and bought tickets to the opera some cars down. The baboons laughed and threw feces throughout Pognafio's entire performance. Terrified and affronted, but being nothing less than the greatest opera singer on the train, he staunchly finished his last scene. When the performance was over, baboons rolled delightedly through the aisles, and Pognafio could never return to the stage.

Every Sunday at noon, the doctors lock Pognafio the opera singer in a small room with three baboons and they all play Chutes and Ladders until the doctors come in the evening. Pognafio has learned to let the baboons win. He has learned patience and many other good qualities. The doctors expect him to make a full recovery.

When all of the equipment is sterilized and cleaned I look closely at the flashes of lamplight reflected in the window. I can see Samuel's elbows and upper arms on each side of the window, his collarbone is the scrubbed wood molding of the ceiling. He has grown vast and my heart swells.

There is a distinctly meat-y smell in the hospital car.

The lion feasts on the leg of an old lady. The old lady is dying of pneumonia. She is asleep and dreaming of running very fast. When she wakes up, she will not wake up. The lion groans with pleasure.

Samuel.

***

I am always waking to the smell of sleep in our compartment. But this time I can feel another sleeper near me. It is the lion, just beneath the bed. I can smell his feral sweatiness, his carrion breath blasting huge tornadoes of plaster dust out from under the bed.

"I told you not to come here," I say, banging my fist on the bed frame, sending out clouds of dust.

He snorts awake, bleary eyed. "There's nowhere else to

sleep," he says, "Besides, you owe me, I saved your life."

I know that the lion is referring to the occasion where it chased me up an air vent in the library car and onto the roof of the train. When it had cornered me against the flashing walls of the tunnel, inches from my ear, I slipped and would have fallen down, beneath the tracks, had the lion not lunged forward to grab my shirt at the last moment.

"That," I say, "is debatable."

The lion scoffs and rolls his feline eyes, inching his massive body out from under the bed. He slinks through the compartment door, leaving it slightly ajar.

The last thing to disappear from view is the mangy tuft on the end of his gnarled tail.

***

Eyes that are exceptionally fit can read the white writing that flashes by every so often on the tunnel walls outside the windows. In only a third of a second, it is impossible to read the whole sentence but fit eyes read a word, if they're lucky, sometimes two. And then they compare notes.

Today the word is mutton. They are talking about mutton in the dining car above the feint swoosh and click of the tracks. The chandeliers swing gently. Red and gold streamers, left over from a birthday party last week, hang from them and twirl in the air displaced by moving bodies walking up and down the aisles of the car, bringing food and coffee and small packages wrapped in brown paper to the other occupants of the boomerang patterned tables.

"All mutton may be lamb, but is all lamb mutton? No," a gentleman says.

Another man has recognized the word extravagant. "Extravagant?" someone questions, obviously skeptical.

The man nods and smiles knowingly, "I always spot the 'e' words, you know that Dolores."

"Yes, but *extravagant?*" Dolores repeats, glancing around the table.

"Mutton is mutton, that's what they say," says another gentleman.

"Extravagant mutton."

I stand, scoop up some of the breadcrumbs from my cheese and fish sandwich, and slide out of the car.

***

In one car there are bluebirds; so many bluebirds that it is impossible to enter any compartment in the car. Bluebirds on top of bluebirds on top of bluebirds crowd every compartment. They sit on windowsills and the floor, they flap over one another in the air, they open the doors and walk around, their little heads bobbing as they chase one another back and forth down the aisles.

When someone enters the car, a few bluebirds have to leave. That is how many bluebirds are in the car. When the person leaves again, the bluebirds fill up the space they leave behind, and jabber enthusiastically.

There is only one man who lives in the bluebird car. His name is Derek and he has lived there for seven years. The bluebirds live with him peacefully, as far as anyone can tell there is no bribery or coercion. The bluebirds build nests in his hair and part when he comes through the door. When Derek leaves the car, he is followed by an impenetrable cloud of bluebirds. The bluebirds that stay in the compartment when he leaves are always sad and passive. The bluebirds are in love with Derek and don't know what to do with themselves when he leaves.

***

As far as I can tell, the lion is discouraged by my rebuke in our

154

compartment. He has not reappeared the whole morning.

Samuel is awake. I know this because the dust billowing from under the door to our compartment is giving off a particular odor. It is the odor of Samuel walking through it. I open the door, white clouds poof outwards and I plunge through them to Samuel, who is dancing in the middle of the room, kicking bright clouds of white plaster dust up off the floorboards.

Dust is falling from the ceiling, from the rattling walls. Dust is trailing out the door and into the aisle of the car, down my throat.

A bluebird chitters nicely in the aisle outside our door. The train rattles.

"I told Derek he could come with us to the Library car," Samuel says. Another bluebird appears in the door, then another and another and in a minute a hundred bluebirds are swarming in a tight knot around a figure. It is Derek.

"Hello, Derek," I say, brushing the dust off of my clothes and hair. My attempts are unsuccessful. Dust stays in my pores and when I brush off the outer layer, the inner layer pushes up through my skin and resettles. Samuel never brushes off the dust. He is white and chalky like a blank canvas. He shakes a bluebird near where Derek's hand would be and we close and lock the door behind us as we leave. Samuel looks at me knowingly. I think he is saying that he knows about the lion under our bed this morning.

Derek seems gloomy.

His bluebirds peep in a passive way.

As we are walking to the Library car, our train passes another train. The air compression is dreadful. Everyone is holding their hands over their ears. The windows flash with other faces in other cars on the other train. The faces are holding their hands over their ears.

Samuel is behind me, holding his hands over his ears. Derek is close after and all the bluebirds are on the ground around us, their wings clasped tightly over their ears.

Derek is not holding his hands over his ears. A pair of bluebirds are nestled against his ears like ear muffs. They are holding their wings over their ears.

Derek smiles at me sadly, then looks across at the other train. The people look the same as us, only there are no bluebirds.

I know that Derek is important to this train because he has moved into the bluebird car. I just don't know how yet.

We will pass this train for a few more minutes, deafened by the clacking of the rails and held in place in the corridor by a constant rush of pressing air until, suddenly, it passes.

Amidst the noise, a bluebird chirps. Derek scoops it up in one hand and strokes its small head until its eyes close. It shoots up into the air and whirls around Derek's head, warbling happily.

There are a lot of other trains in the tunnels and a lot of other people are on those trains, rocketing past other trains and causing their occupants to hold their hands over their ears.

The bluebird chirruping around his head, Derek smiles sadly at me again. Because of all the bluebirds, I am the only one that sees him. Samuel's eyes are squinted shut.

Before I lived in the dusty compartment with Samuel, I lived with Derek in a vestibule, with his three older brothers, all of whom were deaf and sullen. All four of them were named Derek, as far as I could tell, and they had long, silent conversations with each other that I never understood. Derek's brothers, Derek, Derek, and Derek, never seemed to like me very much. I was not offended. We lived in a very small space and it is hard to get along with people in a very small space, especially when there are always other people's coats getting in your way. Derek was much quieter then and sometimes I caught him painting the insides of unoccupied cars.

It is not against any rules to paint the insides of unoccupied cars, but it is not recommended without a special permit. When paint of a certain color is applied to the walls of a compartment, it may or may not attract a great host of mealworms.

The mealworms come in the deep of night, devour the walls with steady, dedicated vigor, and disappear as silently as they came.

It is dangerous to lose a wall in a compartment, and inconvenient, because it will never grow back.

Derek painted many walls. There is even an entire missing car, holding the other cars together on the train by its glimmering steel skeleton. No one goes to the skeleton car except Derek and Samuel and I. When you are stretched out on the whale bone beams of the missing car, staring up through the arched steel roof supports at the grey and drippy ceiling of the tunnel, every so often there is a glimpse of light, a flicker like a neon sign or one of the words written glowing on the tunnel wall. It is the outside, Samuel says, it is outside.

It is much debated whether or not the words written on the walls are directions or warnings or simply nonsense. Samuel says they are directions.

Samuel has been on the top and on the sides of many cars. Some cars have safety rails, some do not. Some cars are blocked off and a person must exit the train and walk along a little ledge on the side of the blocked off car, or else climb up and slither along on top of it. On the top of cars, the tunnel walls rush by fast, inches away.

Samuel has spent days running his toes along the ceiling on the tops of cars. His toes are worn away to stubs. He says they do not hurt him. Samuel says that toes are vestigial. He says that if the train stopped, we could climb off and walk along the tracks.

When Samuel has seen a word written on the wall, it has always been "Soon," "Close," or "Not Far."

When Derek sees a word written on the wall, it is always: "Lonely."

***

When Derek moved into the bluebird car, he left his paints in the vestibule. Now he paints the walls with bluebird feathers, bluebird droppings, bluebird tears, and bluebird blood. Mealworms are not interested in bluebirds. Many bluebirds have died but they still live in peace. The bluebirds are in love with Derek. They do not mind if some of them die, as long as the rest of them are with Derek.

When the other train passes us, Samuel makes the motion that he makes when he is relieved but also very excited, it is a sort of twist-jerk-hop, but with only his arms. It is difficult to describe. He does the motion again and Derek turns his bluebird-obscured face away from us down the passage.

***

Derek, Derek, and Derek, Derek's deaf and sullen brothers, disappeared many years ago under very mysterious circumstances. One minute they were sitting in the Library car reading about career opportunities with Derek and Samuel. Derek and Samuel got up to visit the archaeological section and when they returned, Derek, Derek, and Derek were gone. The books on career opportunities lay open as if the three deaf brothers were just in another section, about to return and pick them up. So Derek and Samuel waited. They waited long into the night and part of the next day before they realized that the brothers were not coming back.

There are many explanations for what happened, Samuel has proposed most of them. But it is widely and silently agreed upon that, with no one seeing them, no one thinking about them, and no one believing, for that short amount of time, that they even existed at all, they simply stopped existing altogether.

This is why Derek moved into the bluebird car. So many bluebirds lived there, and so many knew them, that there was almost no chance that a moment would come where no one was thinking of him. Derek seems to miss his brothers, but he is generally very happy in the bluebird car. The bluebirds have taught him many languages and his life is full of familiar sounds.

***

Samuel is talking about the outside again. He has been talking about it for ten minutes. I am not listening and not responding because the conversation is not with me, it is with Samuel. When Samuel and Samuel talk together, they do not like to be interrupted. "And if we stop, I mean when we stop, when the train slows and then comes to a stop, we can run along the passages with no walls on either side (at least that we can reach), and we can stand for a long time in one place, or maybe get a ride on another train as it passes, where they speak other languages and eat other food...."

It continues. Derek is silent, but his bluebirds are having a heated debate. All that we can hear is cheep cheep chirrup, but it can be discerned from the nature of the chittering that they are arguing about who loves Derek the most.

***

We cross through the residential cars and into another dining car. It is the last dining car before the Library car. No one has ever been to all the dining cars in the train in one day, so no one is really sure how many there are. The train is very long and there are parts of it that often arrive or disappear without notice. Pieces are blocked off, or passed over, sometimes, without anyone knowing. A dining car you go to on Tuesday, will most likely be somewhere else by Friday. All of these changes seem to happen in the night, when everyone except the mealworms are asleep.

Samuel has ideas about how many dining cars there are

and where they go and why. But it is really quite pointless to speculate. No one has ever been able to count them, and no one wants to.

What we can be sure of is that there is only one before the Library car. As the door opens, there is a flash of sandy-colored mange. It is the lion. He has followed us. My anger this morning was obviously not enough to dissuade him from coming to this dining car to set up an ambush. He is hiding under the dark mahogany bench of a booth. A red and gold light swings back and forth gently over the table. His eyes flash from beneath the bench as this light catches them. Derek doesn't notice anything, but his bluebirds do. I exchange a significant look with them. Even if they do not love me, or like me very much, they are as cordial as the next birds to me. This is probably because they know how close Derek and I are and they respect him too much to make a scene. I'm fairly sure this is the reason for their politeness.

Derek might not have seen the lion, but Samuel saw the lion. He is drawing his penknife out of his pocket and opening it slowly. He is trying to defend my honor, but he does not understand the situation. He is just embarrassing himself.

On the train, somewhere, the location changes frequently, there is an old, decrepit circus. People still go there now and then to see the ancient tattooed lady whose wrinkles have preserved the color of her otherwise bleached-to-nothing body art. She is like a tiger made out of a coloring book, when she grabs the old folds of her skin and stretches them for the paying people, it is like she is showing off her stripes. Old men go there for the boy who found the fountain of youth – he is over two hundred years old now. Though his skin was once soft and pink, his arms and legs slim and shimmery, he is pale now, and stretched looking, like a thin white lampshade covering a flickering light.

When the circus was in its prime, people went there every day to see the animals and watch the shows. But all the animals have died or escaped. The ringmaster still tries to conduct the arthritic trapeze artists and the parade of white ponies (most of whom are painted), but when there is no one there, he sits in the center ring of the main show car and kicks his bare feet in the moldy hay, wheeling back and forth in his rickety wheelchair until the clowns bring out tea at noon and they drink a little together in silence.

People think it is too sad to see the circus like it is now, and they want to remember it when it was good. So no one goes there.

Samuel does not understand what it is like to come from the circus, and be followed by the lions, like I am. He has never seen a great thing become bad like I did before I escaped out the window of a dressing room car in my swan-dress. I keep the swan dress in a suitcase under the bed. I have told Samuel that the suitcase contains financial papers. He is not interested in it. When he is gone and I am alone, I pull out the suitcase and pretend that I believe it holds what I have told him it holds. I settle down with my pen and paper in the dust and prepare to go through some important financial information. Then I open up the suitcase and look at the swan dress and remember how its feathers felt, how its tail billows out.

***

Also in the dining car is a fat woman with a shock of orange hair on top of her fleshy head. Pink rolls of fat sway and jiggle with the train's movement. They are like the rolls in a pile of frosting. She laughs contentedly. She sits all alone. A waiter approaches her and bows deeply before whispering in her ear, gesturing to us. It is always like this in the last dining car before the library car. The woman's name is Madam Mural. Madam Mural nods and the waiter beckons us forward. Madam Mural has met Samuel and I many times but it is clear from her somewhat disgusted expression that she has not met Derek.

"This is Derek," I say, trying not to sound defensive, "He lives in the Bluebird car." Madam Mural snorts disdainfully. She is always doing things with disdain, normal things that you would not think could be done with disdain, but Madam Mural does them. She has been known to walk with disdain, to consume food with disdain, to gesture with disdain, and to read with disdain.

Personally, I think that it is quite silly for someone who is morbidly obese to be disdainful of someone else's appearance, especially when that person is only surrounded by bluebirds, and not fat.

I do not say what I am thinking. Madam Mural is very sensitive. We were once sent out of the dining car because Samuel did not notice that Madam Mural was wearing a new brooch.

"I see you have a new brooch," Samuel says sweetly.

"Oh, this old thing?" Madam Mural simpers, "Why, I've had it for ages, just had it polished, which is probably why you noticed it, you sweet boy." Her face puckers into some sort of strange attempt at embarrassed humility. Samuel cringes.

The lion hums in the way it hums when it is feeling playfully aggressive. I can hear it, and so can the bluebirds. In an instant, the bluebirds are still. They no longer flap and trill. They all perch, one on top of the other, against Derek, who stands motionless. With the bluebirds so close around him, more of Derek's shape can be seen than usual. It is like he is wearing a feathery blue snowsuit.

The lion jumps. Samuel, gripping the penknife, shoves in front of Derek and I. Madam Mural screams and her attendants rush forward from the shadows, grip her beneath her flabby arms and bear her out of the dining car and into the vestibule. The lion, pouncing all this while, lands squarely on the penknife in Samuel's hand.

His body slumps forward onto Samuel, who falls back into the blue-bird suit/Derek, and me, holding my breath.

The lion, not realizing what has happened, stumbles a

bit, raking Samuel across the chest with his massive lion claws. In a panic now, afraid, he pants and falls, the butt of the penknife ramming into Samuel's collarbone, and plunging deeper into the lions chest. The collarbone does not break, Samuel is screaming. Madam Mural, in the vestibule, is crying. The bluebirds on Derek are fluttering and tiny blue droplets are cascading down off their feathers and I realize that they are crying, too. Even if Derek could never understand about the lion, the bluebirds on him understand. A small pool is gathering around Samuel. It is a cool magenta color. It is the bluebird tears mixing with Samuel's blood, mixing with the lions. There is a falling feeling in our stomachs. I can see in the eyes of the bluebirds that they feel it too. The lion scrabbles again, trying to withdraw; Samuel is gored. Samuel has stopped screaming.

***

The falling feeling in our stomachs ceases. The train has stopped.

Derek's bluebird-covered arm is urging me up, pulling me away and I follow him. We race through the dining car, shoving past Madam Mural, who has feinted, and her many attendants. From the corner of my eye I can see the lion looking after us, trying to follow, and falling, its huge face next to Samuel's, their cheeks touching like lovers.

We rip through a residential car. People are noticing that there is an uncanny stillness. We are running past them. We run past them.

We are tripping over people and suitcases as we clamber through the luggage car. Derek's bluebirds get tangled in a bicycle and we spend some time extracting them before we continue on. We are running toward the library car. We are running away from Samuel and the lion.

***

I try to remember how exactly Ioletta looked, and how fragrant and beautiful her turtle skin was. She was prickly. All of her features were just like a turtle, only miniature, and mostly obscured because of all of her blankets and ribbons. Our fathers loved Ioletta. She was the baby turtle that was going to save all of us.

***

When we reach the library car, the attendant hushes us. In the library car, no one notices that the train has stopped. The lights are dim and the walls are grey where they are not full of books. The two stepladders on either side of the car are lined with chameleons bearing tiny, white lights. The white lights are secured to them with leather harnesses. Chameleons walk backward and forward over the shelves.

A huge-eyed man is holding one chameleon. He is peering out the window but the only thing he can see is the chameleon and himself reflected in the glass. Through the windows there are no words, through the skylight there are no flashes of light.

Derek looks at me. I look at Derek. I feel a slow panic rising in my ribcage and I swallow it back down. This is the first look that we have shared since the lion died.

***

I first met Pognafio soon after the end of the circus. The ringmaster introduced us. Pognafio is the ringmaster's brother. The ringmaster is my father. Nonetheless, the relationship between Pognafio and myself is ambiguous. When I first met Pognafio, it was in the closet where he plays Chutes and Ladders with the baboons. The ringmaster walked me to the hospital car. We walked in silence. Then I was aware of a presence behind me, but I never knew that the presence was a lion. Pognafio let the baboons win, but he did not let me beat him. He played with uncommon savagery. The board was smeared with the blood of my cardboard playing pieces.

I was always a circus performer. When I was born I was a tightrope walker. In my early youth I was a lion tamer. In my later youth I was a swan. Now, if the circus had stayed, if Pognafio still sang, I would be a swan. I would be covered in the downy softness of the swan dress day and night, like Derek is covered in bluebirds.

The lions never forgave me for leaving them. It is the first time I have thought of the lions since the lion in the dining car died.

***

Derek is pulling violently at the vestibule door at the back of the library car. There is nowhere else to go, this is the last car, the last car on the train. The bluebirds smash themselves against the door; many bluebirds die.

There is a rushing, roaring sound of movement and at first we turn, thinking that the train has started up again, or that it is leaving without the library car. The man with the chameleon steps out into the aisle and looks down the other end of the car. A swirling tornado of bluebirds is careening down the passage. It squeezes into the car and explodes toward us, knocking the light off of the chameleon and the glasses off the man. The bluebirds blast the vestibule door open and speed into the darkness. Their passing takes minutes, the last bluebird stragglers linger around Derek for a moment, surveying him, and then they are gone. Derek is naked. There are no bluebirds around him

But they are swirling just outside in the darkness. By the light of the chameleons, we can see two steps leading down.

Derek grabs two chameleons and puts one on each of my shoulders. They are very warm. Their dim yellow lights burn against my cheeks. I feel suddenly relieved.

165

The tunnel is warm and damp, it is like the inside of someone's mouth. There is a small dripping sound.

Outside the train is covered in barnacles and moss, interspersed evenly. For a while, looking at the outside of the library car, I think about the direction we should go but then it seems obvious, to the front.

***

Walking along the train, outside of it, the walls barely visible in the chameleon light, Derek, the bluebirds from the bluebird car, and I are very small. We walk for a long time. There are cacti and bones decorating the outside of the cars. When we pass the hospital car the eerie echo of Pognafio's whale song reaches us like a secret message. There are no words written on any of the walls, although I can tell that Derek is looking for them.

No other people have disembarked the train. No other people have noticed that it is stopped.

In dark corners of the tunnel I feel things watching me, but it is not the familiar watched feeling of the lion. It is a stranger. It is the second thought about the lion, since the lion died.

***

When we have walked for hours, we reach the front of the train, where some people have been and others have not. The cement seems to rise up in two even bulges from the slightly curved tunnel floor but then the chameleon light illuminates the people. People in bright, beaded saris and long, billowing skirts, their faces lacey and uneven with tattoos, are crying. They are leaning into one another; they are lying on the bulges. The bulges are elephants. The elephants are dead.

I want to ask what happened but I don't. I want to ask if there are replacements on the way, but I think it would be cruel. I think about the lion. It is the third thought about the lion since the lion died.

The skin of the elephants is pinkish and mottled in places, with wiry hair and large, happy freckles.

The crying people embrace us. They embrace the bluebirds and the bluebirds embrace them back. There are wet, sloppy tears everywhere. It is messy.

Some more bluebirds die, from running in to things, but there are so many of them that it is hardly noticeable.

Derek stands to one side. Skirts swirl around with the bluebirds, the loose cool cloth of saris waves and flaps.

***

After some minutes of sloppiness, the grey hide of the elephants begins to expand.

The crying people look afraid. "Run," someone says, "run."

Everyone looks at each other for a moment, exchanging important information. The bluebirds shoot down the tunnel in a hurricane of feathers, carrying Derek's body on their wings. Bluebirds pick up the people in saris and billowing skirts and a cloud of bluebirds and people rushes away from me.

***

After a few minutes there are no bluebirds. The elephants are expanding, they are huge balloons now, blocking off the tunnel all the way across. Their flesh is still warm; it feels living. My cheek is against it.

I look up. There is a wide swath of speckled cloth stretched over a portion of the tunnel. The chameleon's lights are beginning to die. The chameleons grow colder. I think of Derek being carried on bluebird wings, far away and safe down the tunnel.

I can feel the elephant stretching still, expanding. There was a tense silence, but the tense is gone. It is a timeless silence.

There is no more whooshing of wings down the tunnel. The train is dark and gently steaming.

A cool magenta colored stream is flowing along the train tracks beneath the inflating elephants. I run my fingers through it and feel a pulse.

The chameleon lights are extinguished. The cloth above glows faintly. And I realize that it is not a cloth, but a light.

It is the outside.

It is the first thought of Samuel since the lion died.

THE DROWNED BALLET

. ' . ' . ' . .

I.

Maggie and her brother had been in the castle for seventeen years. That was as far back as either of them could remember. For seventeen years they had been searching for the Drowned Ballet.

Clues and signs of its whereabouts often trickled down the stainless steel walls or appeared in dark corners when no one was watching. Often whispers of the Drowned Ballet swept through the forests of fox flowers that grew in the castle.

But despite the numerous vibrations and countless clues, Maggie and her brother did not know where to find the Drowned Ballet, or even exactly what it would look like if they found it. They did not know how long the Drowned Ballet had been in the castle. They were scared to think of what would happen when the Drowned Ballet was gone. And they were scared to wonder if it had already gone.

Maggie and her brother had been within the windowless, stainless steel castle for so long that their skin was papery and translucent. The spidery paths of veins close to the surface of their skin pulsated in unison with the castle's curious vibrations.

After some time Maggie and her brother stopped speaking aloud and began to tell their stories and play their games late into the night by way of a code they had invented that consisted mainly of blinks, winks, and nods.

This was the way that Maggie and her brother spoke in the castle because whenever a loud noise was made, they felt the walls of the castle moan in pain and imagined that the Drowned Ballet was moving further from them.

When they were very young, Maggie and her brother had been taken to see the Drowned Ballet by a person they no longer remembered, in a place that was not the stainless steel castle. They did not remember anything about it, except that they had seen it.

There were many flowers that grew in the castle and all of them had the heads and tails of foxes. The fox flowers covered everything in their path and had been known to bury armchairs, boudoirs, and bureaus.

Often Maggie and her brother picked the fox heads off their stalks and drank the yellow nectar they produced. Drinking fox heads was a favorite thing to do in the evenings in the castle while they walked soundlessly through the stainless steel corridors in search of the Drowned Ballet.

Sometimes days would stretch between the finding of a clue, and the next sign of the Drowned Ballet.

One time it was a month.

When the sign eventually came, Maggie and her brother were almost beginning to believe that the Drowned Ballet was gone.

All of the fox head flowers roared like lions in the darkened corridors. They did not play any games and they only sat together in the stainless steel castle and wondered what would happen next. "Maggie," said her brother in their silent wink/blink language, "I think the Drowned Ballet is gone." But two days later a blue mask was found lying in a pile of rose petals in the antechamber to the main hall, and after that, there was a slipper in the cloakroom.

Maggie and her brother saved the clues that came to them in a large cabinet in the smallest bedroom of the castle.

Maggie and her brother kept the clues in this room because they wanted to keep the fox flowers away from the clues and it was easier to defend a single small space. They ran to the smallest room in the stainless steel castle and they sat among their clues and hints and rumors. Maggie and her brother did this to reassure themselves that the clues they had received of the whereabouts of the Drowned Ballet were real.

Sometimes Maggie and her brother would dress up in the clues and play elaborate games that always ended in the discovery of the Drowned Ballet.

The best clue to ever be discovered was by Maggie in the kitchen late at night. It was a golden bowl full to the brim with red and gold confetti. At first the contents of the bowl looked like normal paper confetti, but as she approached she realized that the confetti was made of extremely small rabbits. The rabbits crawled all over each other in the bowl, cooing softly. As she reached a hand into the bowl, many of the little glittering confetti rabbits leapt out and scattered across the kitchen. Maggie and her brother transferred the remaining rabbits, each no larger than the head of a pin, to a jam jar. They put breathing holes in the lid and tried to feed the rabbits all of the things that they thought rabbits loved. They tried carrots and lettuce and peas and the left over crusts of sandwiches. They tried lemonade and fresh fruit. They even tried to feed the rabbits a fox flower, but the fox head ate all of the rabbits that came near it.

Eventually all of the little glittering confetti rabbits in the jam jar were dead, and Maggie and her brother squished their tiny bodies between their pale fingers to see what they felt like.

Maggie and her brother were sad that they could not keep

the tiny confetti rabbits and they did not understand why the rabbits had not eaten any of the wonderful foods they had given them. They did not know that tiny confetti rabbits could only eat tiny confetti carrots, tiny confetti peas, and tiny confetti fruits. This was why all of the tiny confetti rabbits had died.

Some of the tiny confetti rabbits had escaped capture and imprisonment in the jam jar however, and lived out the rest of their lives eating the tiny confetti foods that grew in the space beneath the refrigerator and behind the water heater in the stainless steel basement. When they grew old they wrapped each other's tiny bodies in bright yellow cocoons and transformed each other into small green butterflies that pollinated the fox flowers in the hallways and the bedrooms of the castle. The small green butterflies sometimes banged their rabbit bodies against the stainless steel walls of the castle, as if they knew that sun awaited them on the other side, but the walls moaned in pain and the small green butterflies fell exhausted to the floor.

When this happened, Maggie and her brother heard the music of the Drowned Ballet receding deeper and deeper into the stainless steel walls, lower and lower in the castle. But when they rushed to the stainless steel basement of the castle, all they found were butterflies and fox flowers.

Sometimes in their dreams, Maggie and her brother imagined that the Drowned Ballet was gone. They imagined that the fox flowers overtook the smallest room in the stainless steel castle and that the clues to finding the Drowned Ballet were buried beneath them forever. Maggie and her brother sometimes woke up with a gasp and looked at each other across the floor of the smallest room of the castle and sometimes one would say in their wink/blink code, "Did you dream that the Drowned Ballet had gone?" And the other would reply, "Did you?"

Another time, Maggie and her brother were walking on the ninth floor of the stainless steel castle, sucking the nectar from two fox head flowers and having a silent wink/blink conversation about the Drowned Ballet when a great, shivering moan shook the castle. It was the loudest moan the castle had ever made and Maggie and her brother shook with fear, so much so that they almost cried aloud in the silence.

Maggie and her brother hurried down the hall toward the sound but when they arrived at the staircase they found a very disappointing clue. It was only a length of blue satin ribbon on the floor, pointing due south.

Maggie and her brother picked up the blue ribbon and hurried due south. But all they found at the end of their path was a dense grove of fox flowers. Beneath these fox flowers were a few of the corpses of the confetti rabbits, but Maggie and her brother did not know this.

Maggie and her brother clutched the blue satin ribbon that had been pointing due south, glad that it had appeared in the corridor to tell them that the Drowned Ballet was near, even if they had not been quick enough to catch it.

One of Maggie's favorite clues had been the nest of lady's shoes that they had found in the early morning. The nest was lined with velvet cloth and set up in a corridor they often walked through. No fox flowers had gotten to the nest yet and all of the shoes, not one looking more than slightly worn, were the right size for her and her brother.

Maggie and her brother kept most of the shoes in the smallest room with the other clues, but they took them out often to try them on and walk around. Their skinny, pale ankles looked like lilies blossoming from beaded satin paddies in the water.

II.

Right now Maggie and her brother are playing dress-up with the clues they have collected in the castle, clues that have not led them to the Drowned Ballet.

Maggie and her brother are playing a game where in the

end they will find the Drowned Ballet that they remember having seen only briefly, a long time ago, led to the location by a series of increasingly promising clues that in real life they will never find or hear, to a place that is in the stainless steel castle where the Drowned Ballet has been waiting to begin, waiting for them to arrive. When they enter the theatre, the dancers will begin to dance and the musicians will lift their dusty violins.

At the end of their game, Maggie and her brother take their seats in the crowded theatre and watch the Drowned Ballet, acted for them in their game by some fox head flowers, a green butterfly, and a pair of beaded satin shoes.

Maggie and her brother are playing soundlessly in the smallest room of the stainless steel castle. The descendants of the tiny confetti rabbits flit past the open door. Fox flowers grow around the hallway outside, peering in curiously, as if they are hoping to grow into the smallest room and bury the clues about the Drowned Ballet that Maggie and her brother have collected – clues they hope will lead them to the Drowned Ballet, which they are watching now, in the game that they are playing.

III.

It has been three months since the last clue was discovered beneath a bathroom sink. It was a hatcheck ticket. The ticket was number 37. Maggie and her brother know that the Drowned Ballet has gone. It rains inside the stainless steel castle. It rains in every room and in every hallway. Walls of water rise up from the stainless steel basement, washing up descendants of the tiny confetti rabbits.

Every creak and every moan of the stainless steel castle sounds like bending and breaking. Maggie and her brother pack the clues into three enormous barrels that they sew together with the tails of the fox flowers. To lash the barrels into a raft, Maggie and her brother harvest all of the fox flowers. It is a fox flower genocide.

The water rises and rises in the castle.

With all of their clues and hints and rumors packed away, Maggie and her brother clamber onto the foxtail raft and wait for the stainless steel castle to bend and break. When the stainless steel castle bends and breaks, an ocean rushes out of all of the floors of the castle at once, carrying them on their foxtail raft out into the starless night.

Maggie and her brother cling to each other with beaded satin shoes on their hands and feet. When the ocean settles they look around for the Drowned Ballet. There is no sign of the Drowned Ballet, until a little green butterfly flutters past.

Then, drawing out two paddles made from bedposts, Maggie and her brother row across the sea toward the Drowned Ballet.

RETURN TO THE SEA

• • • • •
•

Open eyes. The perch is thrashing. I throw it up in the air. The impact on the surface of the water kills it instantly. Its flesh is sinewy, soft and cold beneath the hard, scaly rind.

After days, fish begin to flee at my approach. I sit on the sand island, my skin leaking out its water reserves in the hot sun. Wrinkles disappear. Every morning I must go out further for a perch, further from the island.

This morning a single perch flits away at my approach. A single perch's bubbly wake dusts my face in oxygen. The fish dives off the sandy plateau of the seabed—off the shelf in the near distance. Hovering this close, I feel the pull, the downward spiraling yank of deep currents curving the bed down. The pressure, the chill of the deep steels my limbs and I feel myself drift. Frantically, I turn and pull myself toward the island. For a moment, back turned, I feel my feet slip over the edge, kicking white, crystalline sand into the abyss. Tucked in, I bullet back to shallow water and, a pair of human eyes above the surface, I shudder until the night.

The bare top of the island has the sound of sparkling all over it. Settled there, a distant, gentle wind whistles, tumbling sand particles over sand particles over sand particles. In the sun, the sand whirls in constant motion. At night, all is still and the ocean turns to something magically shimmering, the only sound in the windless waste a lapping sparkle.

***

When I was young my brother bathed me in the sink. A mother too busy even to look at her infant son is always trusting of an intelligent nine-year-old. The first and only child ever to be re-warded, my brother Samuel would take me from my crib and plop me down in the clogging, cloying warm water, my skin would crawl with chills and tremors, fear when the water dashed against the steel sides of the bin, shock when the water cooled to a terror-making forty. He would sit me there for what could have been days, while he rang out sponge after sponge of dirty water over my head, ears and nose filling with liquid, unable to fend off the constant drizzle. A Chinese water torture—a half-state in and out of water and when I cried and mother screeched for silence at a slightly lower octave than my scream, Samuel jerked my feet and slid my fleshy body underwater where I gasped and spluttered, mouth wide, nostrils flared in terror.

And when my look was grey, a half-drowned look, and I was still, Samuel drug me up and wrung another sponge.

That was how I learned to be. To be beneath the waves.

Samuel, though, never was an ocean swimmer.

***

I know that there are predators there—beyond the shelf, in the darkest reaches. So much deeper than my frail limbs could take me; my soft, wrinkly and ballooning skin: permeable and weak. Those other animals don't seem forgiving.

Soon I will be the great emptier and no perch will glide through the soft white sand here. Already they are so scarce. Already I see the other animals, in the periphery, bare flashes and subtle movements in the water. There, over the edge, they feast.

I try to catch a ray—embarrassing levels of failure. The ray slashes through the water like paper cutting through the air. I can blow the thing off course with a wave, but never get it close enough to dry sand. It is too dexterous, too slim and sly. Beneath us is a great, delicate reef. A weaving ocean garden made of stone-hard lace, full of intricate highways and sulfurous alleys. Beneath the island is a hamburger restaurant for tiger sharks. They appear on the periphery, motionless shadows hovering just beyond the darkening of the water, just on the edge of the shelf.

***

In my father's garage after school I am a boy. I have arrived at the house to find a beautiful woman in distress. Watery black lines mar her face. Lips pursed and puffed, hair rumpled, she is crying on the rotating saw table.

"What's up?"

"What's up, yourself," she sniffles indignantly.

My brother's car is gone, my hands are sweaty, the girl's skirt is hiked up. She uncrosses her legs, bony shoulders bent forward. Mary.

***

The white ray I harassed yesterday returns. As he traverses the beach, his small eyes give me the look of tortured souls, the look of sand creatures plied and pulled and rubbed by fate, out searching for an easy end. He hovers at the tide line, inching out. The island shrinks beneath us to encompass myself, the ray, and the edge of the shelf. There is no other space. He beckons, barb tail swinging madly, frantically, outward. He is calling now, toward the shelf, and I am not following.

I kick out, I grab him up and throw him back into the real

179

ocean, off the shelf and as my hand leaves his guttered mouth, his tail dashes into my forearm, a quick wrap and release. The surface of the sun-yellowed skin there erupts into whiteish lumps. My heart races and I plunge in after him, driven by his DNA, over the shelf where I allow myself to be sucked down, dousing the hot numbness, but the arm boils the ocean like a red hot poker and my whole body, submerged in the deep, begins to burn.

My mouth is open when I wake. My stomach is full of salt and sand. A merciful, saintly dead perch is inches from my loose fist.

I can barely break the rawhide-tough skin. The sun has partly cooked him and he tastes like bacteria—like a fungus.

How long have I been in the ocean? How far in the deep have I gone?

I did not expect to see the sun rising from every direction at once when I awoke on this sand bank, in this reef, in this ocean, alone. If, indeed, I had expected to wake, I would have expected to see the night. The long night, the never-ending night. My life has been a life of nights.

Nights spent dressed-up in plastic clothing, stifled and hot.

Nights spent not breathing, beneath the dock in the water, while my brother took woman after woman on the planks above. I watched them, free, in speculative silence, through the slats.

***

My hands pound on the glossy wood rail of the USS Victoria. Her captain steers her south, into a hot breeze. I feel moisture rise from the sea, up from floors below.

"Jump." I say.

"Why?" I ask.

"Jump in. You don't belong here."

"I belong here."

"Don't you want a bath, a wash, a swim?"

"I'll drown."

"Swim."

"The ladders are raised, I can see them. I'll drown."

"Jump in. You can swim."

"I can't swim forever. It's suicide."

"Don't you want a bath, a wash, a swim?"

"I'll drown."

"Swim. Swim away. Swim forever."

"You want a swim, Arthur?" My skin crawls at her touch as Mary runs two fingers along my arm. I brush away the chills and turn, smiling.

Her eyes are dim and grey. I hear my brother's name behind her lips, "Samuel," she is saying when she leans in to me from the rotating saw table in my father's garage, from the wooden rail of the USS Victoria, from the velvet drapes in my office, "Samuel" from the feinting couch in the hall. "Samuel. Do you want a swim?"

"No," I answer, "Just looking."

"You don't have to be so serious, Arthur." Her heart is a room without windows. It is this railing—a ship—it is a small dark cabinet in an empty house where clothes are eaten by moths and boots fold over on themselves, forgotten. She was never wanted by my brother. But I took her.

"Arthur, eat your peas," my mother says, "look at Samuel's plate, Arthur."

***

"I was just thinking about," she sniffs from the saw table, wipes her wrist across her nose, smearing a thin web of snot and mascara across her cheek. She rubs the heel of her palm on her jeans, "I was thinking about how all of my favorite songs are about people who stop loving each other."

"Oh, yeah?"

181

"Yeah, it's true." Her bottom lip is quivering cartoonishly. "I guess I'm not meant to…"

"Shut up, Mary."

***

In the night, Mary's perilous red shoes are cast off. Her hot pink flesh is glowing with sex. I know the whole time she is thinking of the dock. But I am free, invisible, naked, the surface of the ocean is arctic but beneath the surface is an animal warmth, so enveloping and whole that no movement breaks it. I am floating free.

I imagine "Arthur." They are calling on the ship, "Arthur." The nets, the life-preservers, the crewmen leaping into the shadowed depths, bright white flashlight beams cutting through the speckled water. Her voice is saying "Arthur," but her heart is saying "Samuel."

"Look at your brother's plate, it's spotless. Don't you want to be like your brother, Arthur?"

***

The shelf is so much darker today. The blackness seems nearer. Is the island shrinking? Am I to be cast into the abyss? I wonder if I could see the colors of the reef beneath us with my wide eyes open and burning. I wonder if, from above, my island is a member of an infant chain, one day to be volcanoed into living land with crawling things and unhappy tourist's children, everything shrouded in a humid cloak of highly-oxygenated air, beneath an umbrella of jungle foliage two miles thick in all directions, isolated from this explosive ocean breeze.

Waves are rising. I know that beneath the surface it is silent, calm, and cool. I have not touched the water's edge in days. The darkness of the shelf looms up toward me. I know

I could wade, I could swim the periphery, but the sand floor seems to slant. And the lace-work, so fragile and willowy. Hollow bones. Bird bones. They could snap at any minute and tumble me, the island, and the ray, into the cold, lightless, airless night. I grow afraid to move. My flesh begins to rot and pillow out.

***

I am a boy when this woman appears before me in the bathroom. My brother has been with her in his bedroom. Her thighs are as thick and fat as my whole torso, glistening with sweat and hard as rocks. I am standing at the toilet, hanging out of my jeans, when she lifts up the pleats of her navy blue skirt and says, "Now you wanna see mine?"

***

On the railing, Mary's red shoes are stabbing the earthy darkness of the deck. "Let's go to bed, darling," she says, puffing up her lips in a ruby donut, and blowing a smoke ring over my face. "I need beauty rest." She steers me by the arm, past the deck chairs and down into the 9-12 elevator block. We have been married seven years and for eleven years, my name has not been Arthur.

I have no name. I am a habitat for sand particles.

When the neighbor girl kicks her bracelet into the murk of the lake, who is the narrow-shouldered boy who sifts through every particle of sand on the lake bottom until its plastic beads catch on his fingers? Go ahead and drop it one more time for twenty dollars. I will catch it. Fools, I could always stop my breath at will.

With no breath, rays and perch drift over the edge of the abyss and gather to me. I am becoming stationery. I am becoming habitat. I am becoming a wave.

When I was on the island, my skin was hot, red and boiled, blisters brewed deep beneath the surface and erupted in yellow, pussy circles, enflamed and infected. It was time to return to the sea.

What is a dolphin, or a whale? Just something that returned like me. My skin grows as hard and slick as the giantess's thigh.

It is hours since I have drawn breath and my heart is slowing to a rumble, no longer a beat.

When Mary came to me on the saw table, her thighs were wet and slippery and I tried to grab her by the ribcage, lift her up and throw her back, but as my fingers forced her body upward into the dark, her fingers lashed back, a quick wrap and release and where her skin touched my skin, the disease was sewn and there was no cure.

THE BRIDGE

. • • • .

Coming over the water, the clearest object on the horizon is the bridge that juts out of one loping hill and penetrates another. It's a suicide bridge, low cement barriers, a thousand foot drop to train tracks, a car dealership, a highway. Some more ancient people here see hundreds, maybe thousands of bodies crowded in the area below, every time they come over the water.

I see one. Or two.

The few that have warranted news coverage. The few that made a romantic piece. Rather than another pathetic mystery, a troubled junkie, a guilty criminal, a desperate prostitute.

One guy with two families in the same city, each unaware of the other. Two names. Four children. Two houses and a winter cabin on Mt. Hood. Three minivans and a pair of ski-doos. Two jobs, even, CPA and environmental studies professor. Two personalities. Apparently, he slept twenty-seven minutes each night. The perfect double-life and no one suspected a thing. Except his seven-year-old girl—split personality, hallucinations, violent outbursts.

One man, left by his wife of seven years. This guy with more than just a passive family history of suicide. In the news story, the mother says the father passed, in the same way, at the same age to the month. And the grandfather. And the great grandfather. No one ever told the boy. Twenty-nine. Two children. One daughter. One son.

Just over the water, when it's raining, each rain drop, close up, looks like a body. For those watching, bodies rain from the bridge day and night. I am watering the tomato plants on the porch, watching rough brown cedar planks grow slick and black beneath the planters. I am watching the neighbor watch the bridge from just over the water. He is standing up, with a pirate-style telescope, tarnished bronze, retractable. The neighbor senses me watching and does a Donald Duck: "Wahk wahk wahk." The neighbor and his wife are voice actors for a local animation studio. He sits on his porch, about seven yards from mine, every morning, drinking coffee from a "World's Biggest A**hole" mug, with the telescope and his newspaper. When he catches me staring, he makes faces, inappropriate gestures, weird sounds. He's making a face now. "Another one bites the dust."

"Really?" I say, glancing at the cloud-shrouded hills across the water. "You saw someone?"

"Nah!" he says, taking a formidable chug of his coffee, tossing the telescope onto the sun-bleached cushion of the patio bench behind him. "Gotcha!"

I force a laugh and dump the rest of the water out through the top of the can. Across the water, the bridge is barely visible, just a little line wavering between two hillcrests, buried beneath veil upon veil of encroaching mist.

On his drive to work every morning, my best friend Charlie passes under the bridge. He's never caught a single disaster and he's been commuting the same way for six years. He is seeing a girl named Lorraine and she's "powdering her nose."

"People seriously say that?" I ask, bending the straw from my whiskey and soda into a little loop, tucking the ends together, forcing them into one another with a squeak.

"It's old-fashioned," says Charlie, "I like it."

"Yeah. Old-fashioned."

Lorraine slips into the booth next to Charlie, her bare thighs make a flatulent rubbery sound as she scoots across the bench. I smile. Lorraine glances at my straw loop and raises an eyebrow. "Lorraine," I say, "are you old-fashioned." Lorraine makes a "chuh" sound, pursing her high-gloss lips.

Charlie shrugs. "Anyway, dude, I doubt that suicides from that bridge are even remotely as common as you think."

"Yeah, have you been up there lately? There's like a wreath every three feet. And I told you, the girls at the dealership…"

Lorraine is rolling her eyes. They're huge and bulbous, like a pug's. I smile again. "You guys are weird," she says breathily. Charlie rubs her bare shoulder, presses his nose into her cheek. "Oh god, Charles," she says, rummaging through her enormous, shapeless red purse. "There are a lot of oils on your skin." She turns to me, gives me a look.

Outside, September wind is barreling through the trees. Lorraine screams and tucks the sleeves of Charlie's sports jacket into her armpits. The jacket won't reach all the way around her ridiculous rack. And she didn't bring a coat of her own. It's old-fashioned. Charlie likes it.

From downtown it's hard to see the bridge. At night the sky purples with city lights and the hills can be identified as a band, a colorless void, speckled with a few glimmering lights like campfires of shepherds in the most remote distance. City lights downtown make people's faces pale and wan. Everyone who passes us looks sick. Lorraine mentions that she is sure she's getting sick. Charlie says they had better turn in then. Lorraine looks pleased. Charlie shrugs and pecks me on the cheek. I smile at Lorraine's open-mouthed stare. She narrows her eyes. She's watching me. Then they both flip their hair over their shoulders and whirl into a passing crowd of people.

"Spare a dollar."

"Nope."

"Any change?"

"Sorry."

"Hey miss, I just need…"

"Sorry, man."

"I bet you have a nice warm bed to…"

"I can't help you."

"I've been on a bus since Friday, I'm trying to make my brother's…"

"Good luck."

When I reach my own street my feet are aching. Someone is waiting for me on the porch. The light is not on, so they've been sitting very still for a long time. Or else they've taken out the sensor. Or else they broke the light. I stand on the sidewalk, looking up the rickety wooden stairs to the shadow in the moldy armchair to the left of my door. Homeless guys don't often make it all the way out here. We're a good three miles from downtown. A forty-five minute walk. Longer if it's a shuffle, not a walk.

While I'm standing on the sidewalk, a dark cloud of equally retarded choices forms in my mind. Going to the creepy neighbors' or walking on and calling my boss, Robbie, who lives about five minutes up the road. I've seen Robbie in his underwear at this hour plenty of times and the last thing I want to see after a night on the town with Lorraine is a lumpy package in a pair of embarrassingly mottled tighty-whitey's. I swivel and as I swivel the porch light clicks on and a body unfolds from the armchair, stretching.

I exhale. "Hey, Haley, you scared me for a sec."

"Oh, sorry, I think I fell asleep." He's dressed in a sort of frilly, blue dress. When he stands, it's obvious that it's a quincienara gown, complete with brilliant spangled sash reading: "Quincienara."

"Whoa," I say.

Haley chuckles like it's a long story. I switch on the lights inside and throw down my bag by the door. The fridge squeaks open—Haley rummaging through some vegetables in plastic bags. "Do you mind if I eat something?"

I shake my head. Haley's brother is a metro police officer. He specializes in crowd control. In the eleven years he's worked for the force here, he's been to about nineteen suicides. Nearly two per year.

"I was on the train once, man, and we got stopped because a sucker splatted on the tracks. Messy."

"That's sick," I say. Haley squirts the empty ketchup bottle for effect, spraying red glop and some flakes of crystallized ketchup goo from the lid in a halo around a piece of cauliflower. The bottle makes a "poot" sound. "That's also sick."

When we are fucking, I lean my head back and stare at the band poster hanging right over the bed. "Xiu Xiu with Jenifer Car and Black Eye. Mississippi Studios" in narrow black and gold letters over a washed-out black and white landscape with lots of static and the silhouette of a kid. Haley's eyes are closed and he's biting his top lip. The landscape is the view of the West Hills from over the water and there's the faintest little grungy line, connecting two shallow peaks.

Haley comes, moans, and shivers. I slide onto the floor. Haley rolls over, opens my laptop and logs on. The password is the name of my cat. He guessed it eleven months ago.

"You can't stay here tonight," I say, spreading my legs out on the itchy wool carpet, resisting the urge to scratch. The itchiness feels good.

"You hog the bed anyway."

"It's my bed."

Haley rolls onto the floor and crawls over to his quincienara dress. "Can I borrow some pants, though?"

In the morning, the creepy neighbor is sitting with his wife on the front porch. They both have retractable telescopes. The wife is looking through hers, the "World's Biggest A**hole" mug clutched in her left hand. The husband is slouched back with his telescope between his legs. "Lots of birds this morning," the wife says.

The husband winks at me, extends the telescope slowly with the eyepiece tucked in his crotch. Extend, retract, extend, retract. He says "Argh" like Popeye and takes a gulp of coffee. I shudder. Lock the front door. Lock the screen door. Robbie honks.

Robbie has been delivering sandwiches downtown since he was fourteen years old. His dad owns the whole chain. For some reason he lets Robbie manage the downtown shop. He's been thirty-three years in December working for Loafer. Working for his pa. Robbie's seen five scenes under the bridge. He never saw a body, he says, but once he saw a shoe. He struggles with the heater button on the dash and swerves into the middle lane of traffic. Someone honks. "Goddamn heater. That shoe bummed me, man. It really bummed me."

Robbie hits the little black button and the icon pops to red exactly seven seconds before he pulls up to Loafer and shuts the car off. "Shit man. It's freezing."

"You can go in and warm up," I offer, "I'll put out the signs."

About a week ago an old guy comes in, orders a sandwich and sits by the window in the only red plastic booth. Another old guy joins him. They're both well-dressed, their shoes are shined, they have matching pink carnations in their button holes. When I bring out the first sandwich, I ask the second guy if he'd like anything. He smiles, opens his mouth and lets out a horrible, breathy moan. It's barely discernable as a moan of dissent. I nod a little, caught off guard. The man moans again, a rattling, spit in throat sound.

"Please, excuse my brother ma'am. He don't need a thing."

I am staring. I look at the floor and mumble, "Do you need anything else?"

There's no lunch rush at Loafer, but a steady trickle. The second old man leaves. The first is still sitting in the red booth. He cleans his hands with a mini-towelette and scratches his beardless chin for over an hour. Robbie is slicing cheese in the back when the first old man comes back up to the counter.

"Hey, can I get you something else?" I say.

"No." He clears his throat. "I know you meant nothing by it. It's no harm. I seen you looking over at my brother." He smiles warmly, the whites of his eyes glisten.

"My brother hasn't spoke since our father killed himself in 1992. He jumped right off that bridge. We were all crossing together. He jumped right off and left my brother and me, left us up there. My brother had a trauma in his life and he don't speak on account of it." He scratches his chin a little and rubs his hand on the red-tiled countertop. From the spot where his hand touches down, a small halo of warm fogginess appears. "I'm sorry to mention, but you seemed…"

Color rushes to my cheeks.

He smiles. "You seemed troubled. It's no thing to be troubled by. We're all happy now."

I can feel blood in my face doing embarrassing and obvious things.

"Good day, ma'am," he says.

I tell Robbie I am going to walk home but instead I walk up toward the hills. It's not far. Nothing is far in this city. I think about going to the grocery store. I think about stopping at Charlie's office. I think about getting a drink at a bar I like right up the street a little ways. I don't need any groceries and this store is pretty overpriced, also I don't want to talk to Charlie about how he banged Lorraine nine times last night. I stand outside the bar for a long time.

It is the place where I met Haley. He was tending bar. He made me a whiskey and soda before I could tell him what I wanted. I thought he looked smart. He thought I looked lonely. I realize after a while that my eyebrows are curled together. I don't like whiskey and soda.

My feet carry me up Madison Street, the sidewalks are wavy red brick with golden plaques every ten feet or so, the names of donors stamped in small font, all partially obscured by leaves and trash. I see the name Charles a few times. I stop in front of one plaque. It says "anonymous donor" in all lowercase letters.

The wind is picking up again. A man on a skateboard veers off the sidewalk to avoid me and out into traffic. I watch him weave through cars effortlessly before he disappears over the crest of the hill.

I think about going back to the bar. I think about walking back to the bar that Haley works at now, but I'm wearing my faded red Loafer t-shirt with my name sewn on the pocket.

I stop in the middle of the bridge and look down. The cement rail is low enough to get my knee up on and the view is beautiful. I lean against the rail, my back to the city, facing the mountain and the highway, gaining altitude in the distance until it seems like it's parallel to the bridge. The road curves out of sight. My phone buzzes in my jeans pocket and I pull it out. The battery is almost dead. A text from Charlie: Ha ha, Lorraine thinks you r a creeper. Knew a jumper. LOL."

Another buzz. Charlie says: Not LOL jumper. LOL you a creeper. Ha ha.

A semi passes, close to the sidewalk. The diesel gust of wind that follows it nauseates me.

On the way home I pass the streets where Charlie, Haley, and Lorraine work. I pause at each one.

As I cross over the water, dark grey autumn clouds crowd the sky and everything except the skyscrapers on the opposite bank are invisible. I wait out some hail under an oak tree and slide my broken coat zipper up and down the left side of my coat. The buildings look like broken fingers reaching up through the mist off the river. Some specks of humans are fishing off the retaining wall, slowly being swallowed by rain.

THE RIVER

Some floods are worse than others. The flood when I am fourteen is a flood that takes away every single fence in the field, levels the irrigation creek with silt where we used to fish for catfish and collect tadpoles in the summer. The flood comes fast, sometime in the night when Mom and father are asleep and I am in my room, head pulled under the sheets looking at a dirty magazine I bought off a kid at school whose name I don't remember. But I remember the acne all over his neck, feeling lucky when I look at him despite the fact that he's got a grown brother who'll buy him smut and booze and cigarettes. The dog is curled up in the empty crook of my legs, head on my ass.

The flood when I am eight washes in a playground of old rusty construction equipment, a gnarled mass of steel, mysterious wheels and spokes, an old car horn that hoots an apologetic, watery sound. The heap is a perfect house; it has a crow's nest, a dungeon, a kitchen and a cockpit. When I climb it I feel tall for the first time. The dog is a puppy and we play lonely on the junk heap together until my father and my Uncle Dan drive in with Rodriguez's big backhoe. And they break the whole thing down. They pack it up.

The flood when I am nineteen almost drowns the dog. She is paddling toward the rowboat, off the hill turned island where the cows are all scrunched up tight together moaning like they're seeing their lives flash before their eyes. The dog's eyes are wide and hot, the white's clear and visible from where we are, rocking gently, rowing slow to meet her. She goes under. The whole flood's no more than ten feet deep anywhere, barely laps at the edges of the highway by the house that winds through the valley, barely reaches into the neighbor's chicken coop leaned against the side of their house. But my father's hand flashes out to grip my arm, fingers digging in the fleshy part above the elbow and he says: "Let her go," and I say no, pull without thinking. "Let her go, son," he says, not tender. My foot's dug in and I am watching for her nose to break the surface, watching for her head to come up shaking and my father's other hand reaches round and slaps my face. I see stars and no bubbles or air rising. When we reach the highway, my father lugs the rowboat over the guardrail alone and I remember what has been taken from me in these two over-long decades. A shape is loping through the near-night mist toward us. We hear a strained bark, and the clatter of the dog's toenails on wet cement. The dog is alive and running into my arms. My father laughs.

When I am eleven there is no flood, though the grass in the center of the field is a mud pile where the neighbor kid and I wrestle hard in September. His angry spit breath puffs into my face and I throw him down, step hard on his wrist until we hear a crack and I am too stunned to step off, too stunned to back away and I just stand there listening as his laughter crescendos into a scream so loud both our mother's ears start to burn a half mile away and the dog starts running to us.

When the flood comes in November, I am fifteen and I am at Michaela's house, my face buried so deep in her hair the television which plays late night cartoons is invisible. Michaela's little brother is invisible. Michaela's face is invisible. All that is visible is an ambient glow, punctuated by wide slats like prison bars over a white hot light. I am not ambitious. I will never reach the out-of-focus bars. I will never stroke the ambient glow. Michaela's little brother swears. Michaela laughs. Her laugh is a rumble through the hair prison. I nestle farther in and the phone rings. My mother, panicked, screeching. The horse, Pepper is in the field. Water is coming. Pepper is in the field. Father is in Bend and Pepper is in the field and my Uncle Dan's at the hospital with Norma. Help help, Pepper is in the field.

I run home in the rain. Pepper's head and neck are barely visible above the water, close to the highway. She has done a thing that horses do when they are in too much pain, her body has shut down except her eyes which flit wild from mother to me to mother to me to the dog like we are her executioners and she is not guilty and she would tell us to spare her if she only spoke our language.

We are not your executioners, Pepper. It's all alright. It's all alright as I reach down with my pocket knife in my left hand, feeling with my right along her twisted legs, wrapped so tight in the wires of the fence that the wires are flabby trenches in her skin. It's all alright as I dig into the trenches and Pepper's body spasms and spasms but she is too exhausted to move, can't fill her giant lungs for the pressure. It's all alright I say as I dunk my head under but it's night and it's too dark to see anything. It's all alright I mutter to Pepper, and my mother, and the dog, and the ambient light and the prison of hair and the saint-like glow of Pepper's shimmering horseshoe turned up facing me from the muddy field turned lake bottom. I break my head out of the water and click the pocket knife shut and don't look at my mother as I take the shotgun from her hand and Pepper, we are your executioners.

The dog barks after the shot, goodbye.

When the flood comes and I am sixteen, my father and mother are in Bend with Uncle Dan, burying Norma with her mother and her infant son under dead grass in an unkempt cemetery where Norma's family bought spaces back when they had money and a summer home, the hope of grandchildren, great grandchildren, and a long and happy future. Norma is bitter my whole life, dreaming constant waking dreams of who her dead baby would have been. Toward the end, she sees him in me when I bring them baskets of food from mom and I stop visiting, I start avoiding Uncle Dan who suddenly seems to see the dead baby too when he sees me or else he sees his dying wife see me. And he shivers all the time and he scowls at me.

I am sixteen, I am always with my cousin Francis. Francis's whole body is a landmine that I fall on voluntarily about every two seconds when we're together. When we were young, we rode around, we chased the dog together, we shot at pigeons and ducks and squirrels with aim so poor houses miles away could feel the pepper of our shots. We make love a lot in the groves of cottonwoods on my Uncle Dan's land, land he leased to this corporation so they would plant these rows of barrel-round trees in lines so even and straight they are walls in the summer. Francis wants to pretend she has no parents so we make like we are the last people on earth and we've only just found each other after sixteen years of wandering. It feels sweet to me because it feels like the truth but Francis' fat thighs and round stomach are all Francis thinks is sweet. When we get close we drift apart. That is when the flood comes: when we are in the trees, having animal sex like two puppies who don't know how to do it but want to try so hard and don't care if they look silly trying.

The ground gets soft, then wet, then wetter, then in fifteen minutes, we are three inches deep. We run barefoot through the pastures and Francis steps on some barbed wire and we keep running. Cow shit water cleanses Francis' wound but it's too late. By the time my parents return, Francis is dead of Tetanus and I am moody, feeling imprisoned, guarded. Like if I say something, I'll have to mean it. Not sure I mean anything. Feel like I'll never say aloud what a person means to me, if it means I have to really feel something.

When I am six the water comes strong in right on my birthday. My mother watches the sun set over the flood with me in the crook of her arm, skin enclosing me and I peer through the tangled strands of her hair at an ambient sunlight, striped by strong bars of grayish brown and I feel like I never want to look out, really again. The familiar landscape of my memory is washed away, flooded out. "Is it the ocean?"

"No baby, it's the river."

GLORIA

No birds sing in this part of the forest. There is no sound of rollicking wildlife, no shivering undergrowth. No wind moves the dark leaves of the canopy. No fresh air at all has penetrated this part of the forest and what air manages to squeeze itself through the heavy branches and graying pine needles is gelatinous and difficult to breathe.

Laboring with the stagnant atmosphere, his feet disturbing little plumes of tree dust and brittle four-autumns-past leaves, is a man with the pinched expression of a starving jackal and the neck of a sickly, colorless giraffe. The man puzzles over a tree, moves on to a bush, then across a small clearing to another tree. No great light is coming down through the trees, though it is a cloudless day, and his jackal features are only as obvious as the vague, shallow lines of split bark on the beech trees he grazes with anxious fingers.

Years ago, each tree and bush seemed distinctive and unique. The character of the plant life radiated out of each separate needle, forming a pathway from the road where he has parked his decrepit CRV, to the familiar grounds of his youthful wanderings. He is aggravated by the absolute sameness of this once distinct foliage. But he is also relieved. His fierce canine expression slackens and his face returns to its customary calm. Head wavering on his prodigious, pale neck, he puffs out his cheeks and blows a raspberry in the silence.

If any of those cohorts from his youth—the ones who knew, as he once knew, the tight and claustrophobic inches of the forest like the backs of their hands—could see him now, he would have been a stranger. They would, however, despite the unkind effect of the years that separated them from him currently, have most definitely recognized his previous jackal-like expression. A look like that is unforgettable.

Fortunately for him, all of those people who might once have been able to identify him, all of those people who knew the forest once, who knew him once, are gone. No one has a chance of navigating the deepness of this forest. No one except Steven.

***

Tree shadows have followed him as he speeds down the wet highway, cutting a line from the Mackley Park turn-off through a haze of thin rain and a half-hearted fog straight to the bedside of his father-in-law.

***

"Dennis, she looks up at me every day. She looks up through that moss when I call her. You don't know how cold her eyes are now."

Dennis's father-in-law, Steven, has been cloistered in the Lakewood Valley Assisted Living Facility since the age of twenty-seven. Steven suffers from an intense and debilitating paranoia that surfaced in his youth. His madness culminated in a string of arsons, for which he was arrested. When he admitted to his legal counsel that a sinister man who had been following him forced him to burn the houses, he was deemed incapable of governing himself, and implanted in the home.

Despite this seemingly insurmountable handicap, Steven has dedicated himself to the study of science and natural philosophy. Years ago, Dennis's visits to the private apartment in Lakewood were like free tutelage. Steven's wise and lonely ramblings, interrupted only occasionally by fits of oblique terror and rage, were Dennis's only stimulation in a world now devoid of the rages and terrors he had himself known as a youth.

When true and honest madness began to manifest in Steven it took weeks for Dennis to notice. Now it is difficult to discern any remainder of the former man in a steaming pool of insanity. Only once every few visits does some clairvoyant and beneficent pronouncement make its way past his father-in-law's cracked, trembling lips revealing that a man is sequestered within, as the mad man which houses him is sequestered in the Facility.

Dennis no longer bothers to knock on the apartment door, the stoop of which is overgrown with tangles of morning glory vine and slick with the pulpy remains of twenty or thirty newspapers. Slipping in the newspaper puddle and cursing the neglectful staff, Dennis shoulders the door open and steps inside. The whole apartment smells of medical supplies and dampness. There is probably mold growing in the walls. Mold abounds here, in this complex, and in the town. Every man-made structure is its sporing ground, every dark place its little chapel. Covering his nose and mouth with the sleeve of his jacket as he passes the filthy, cramped restroom, Dennis walks straight across the bedroom to the window. "Steve, it's so muggy in here, you tell them to open the window when they come." He shoves open the high window which shudders as it moves in its uneven aluminum frame.

His father-in-law lays prostrate on the bed, strapped down beneath soft, beige sheets, breathing heavily into his pillow. Dennis takes a seat near the bed, in a rickety folding chair that has almost grown into the worn carpet. Steven moves his head left and right. The creases in his neck and face stretch into faint lines, then fold back into papery, elephant skin. Outside the window, children scream and laugh. A gunshot rings out far off in the distance, somewhere in the forest near where Dennis recently wandered.

"I didn't want to tell you, Dennis but I'm in love." Dennis reaches out to hold the withered fingers in their cotton-lined cuff. "I'm in love with her, I have been for years. She comes in here to see me. I never leave, you see. I can't." The hand jerks away at Dennis's touch. The whole bed jumps as the strap pulls at the bed frame. "I'm in love, don't you get it? Can't you comprehend you ignorant, fascist swine. You limaceous endomorph, you zeophyte, you placenta." Steven yells angrily for a moment and is calm. Dennis's eyes unfocus, the whole room is a beige, antiseptic blur. The bed is a raft, the children peering in through the window, holding themselves up by their elbows, are trying to get a good look through boiling waves of brownness. With his eyes squinted up and strained, they look like dogs, their jaws slavering, eyes wide and pupil-less. Other gunshots ring out, some closer, some farther up the mountain-side. Old men out hunting the coyotes with their sons. Dragging huge, rotten carcasses through the undergrowth to leave the scent of death behind them.

"I went there just yesterday, Dennis," Steven says, suddenly cogent and bright-eyed. He snatches Dennis's hand and grips it tightly. "The nurse who comes here, she's a witch. She leaves my bonds loose so I can slip right out. I think she pities me. She's a whore, too, I've seen her. I followed her to the spot. You know the spot I'm talking about. Right? You know. They all know." The children cackle from the window. Dennis wants to shoo them away, to rise and show them that he is not a corpse, but Steven continues, "I went there to see her. I owed her that much for never speaking. She was so beautiful. She was so thin. She was so damn cold. I know now why you told me...something like that can weigh on a man, I know. I know

now. Aren't you glad?"

Dennis nods. He is not glad. He does not like those children hearing this revelation, however insane and disjointed it may sound. He rises from the chair but before he can make a movement for the window, they have yelped and retreated. A moment passes and they resume their game out of sight. Another gunshot.

***

People seem more concerned when a body blossoms in roadside foliage, than when it sinks and fails to resurface. In one version of events, the failure of the body to resurface was proof of her immediate ascension.

***

In the kitchen, surrounded by his wife's collection of ceramic roosters and a wide expanse of busy rooster-themed wallpaper, Dennis jabs his fork into a potato. He imagines the potato screaming, writhing beneath his powerful incisions.

"Daddy?" Dennis jabs again, prying apart the papery brown skin to reveal the flaky, pulsing flesh beneath. A cloud of steam breaks over his face. "Daddy? Are you okay?"

"Dennis, stop violating that potato and eat your dinner before I take it away." Nothing aggravates Dennis more than when his wife addresses him like a child. She has no business talking like that to him, or to anyone. Gloria is far past needing to be threatened and chastised. Not that she ever needed discipline.

His daughter smiles at him and puts her soft hand on top of his. Dennis's wife clicks her tongue disapprovingly. "What's up?" Gloria says. She is the most beautiful child he has ever seen. At the age of five, they had thought she could never be prettier but she has only grown more stunning in the decade since, her face blossoming around the twin anther of her radiant brown eyes like a real bayou lily. Her beauty is complimented by a single dimple in her left cheek, a square but not masculine chin, a lineless and peach-smooth forehead, and an untamable head of perfect golden curls which are now pinned up in a light cascade by a little silver headband. Now, as is happening with increasing frequency, she looks more like her namesake than her mother or her father. More like her namesake than any other living being. Dennis's skin twitches involuntarily and his wife snaps, "I mean it, Dennis.

What was the story about the woman intellectual, the succubus who poisoned her husband's second wife with two drops of her corpse cold blood? Did that blood penetrate the fertile womb of the innocent, ignorant female? Was the resultant child angelic or demonic?

Dennis, ignoring his wife's persistent disapproving babble, grips his daughter's hand and pats it lovingly. "Nothing's wrong, sweetheart. I was just thinking about your grandpa." Dennis observes his wife stiffen slightly. She has not seen her father in four years. The last visit was so painful and humiliating that she has refused to continue seeing him. I'd rather, she says, remember him as a real person than a skeleton spewing nonsense and insults to an empty room. She hates that Dennis sees him, hates when Dennis mentions him, most of all she hates when Dennis talks about him in front of Gloria. Her grey eyes grow steely and dark. Gloria smiles sadly and nods, as if she understands. As if her huge, reflective eyes house as deep a vat of sadness as they sometimes appear to house.

When Gloria has been installed in her bed and kissed by both her father and mother, Dennis's wife pours a tremendous glass of whiskey and hands it to her husband. "Thanks, Kat."

They sit in the living room in silence, trees outside the large bay window barely illuminated by a sliver of a moon, thick branches unsuccessfully muffling the continued sound of gunshots on the mountainside. "Still hunting?" Kat says in response.

"I guess it's the only way to be sure," Dennis says, heaving himself to his feet to peer out the window into what he knows is just complete darkness. "I was out there today, but I didn't hear anything," he mutters mostly to himself but Kat, nose in her own glass, hears him and snorts.

"You were what?"

"I was out, you know, where we used to go."

"I hope by 'we' you don't think you are referring to myself, Dennis." Hidden by an overwhelming amount of disdain is a hint of fear.

"No, dearest, I was not referring to you."

Among the glassy reflection of roosters, he can just make out the small flashes of light from rifles firing in the dark, separated from their cracking reports by full seconds, two seconds sometimes three.

***

They almost lived there, out in the woods. Which is foolish. There is more mold there, more rank decay and stagnant water than anywhere else in the town. It is infested. It is filthy.

But to them, it felt open and clean.

Boys in masks and costumes flee through the brush, their capes and shoelaces tangling in nettles and blackberry bushes, spores suck down into their lungs as they struggle with the undergrowth while he watches.

***

In one version of events she is alone in her room at the top of the stairs, looking out into the garden when a moon god with heaving chest and naked limbs slithers out of the hedge and in one swift movement, mounts the rose trellis and knocks on the glass of her window. When she wakes, she leaves with him and never creeps back down the stairs again.

***

When Dennis wakes next to his wife, his immediate reaction is to recoil. Two huge, intently staring black eyes have replaced her small, watery grey ones which, in the morning, are usually squinted with sleepiness and slightly grumpy. The momentum of his initial recoil sends him out of the bed and onto the floor where he lands, legs tangled into an immovable knot of sheets. His breath comes in short gasps as he fights with his feet, waiting for the alien face to peer over the side of the bed but no face appears, which terrifies him more. After a minute of silent struggle, Kat's familiar groggy face slides into view. She laughs. "Were you awake?" Dennis asks, his heart pounding.

"I am now, geez, what did you do?"

Dennis watches his daughter back the car down the driveway. When she reaches the end he goes to meet her, pulls open the heavy driver's side door and pats her head. "You're getting better."

She looks at him very seriously. "You don't have to worry. Everything will be alright, you'll see."

More gunshots echo faintly through the valley.

Dennis pulls into the parking lot of the town's only bar and sits in his car for a while. Eating breakfast here alone is better than enduring his wife's moans and wails about the various chores and tasks he has neglected over soggy bacon, dry eggs, and stale toast at home.

"They're really going after the Keye-Oats, huh?" a filthy, plaid-shirted man says at the next booth. His friend stirs a small dish of mayonnaise slowly with a French fry, "'Spose," he responds.

"But then what can they do? It's the only real way to be sure."

His friend grunts and continues stirring the mayonnaise.

"You know what they say when some animal gets a taste for human flesh?"

The friend's blank stare focuses a little and he pulls the fry out of the mayonnaise. He places the fry delicately between his lips and sucks off the mayonnaise before dipping it back into the dish.

"I read some about these tigers in Bombay all ganged up, kilt four hundred people and the natives had to go and call this English hunter name of Laney. He took care of that bitch. Was sick, they said. Something went wrong with it."

The friend grunts again, "Ain't nothing wrong with a Keye-Oat been eatin' babies. In their blood, isn't it. Scavagers."

"You mean scavengers."

"What I said. Nothing wrong."

The first man shakes his head. "You listen here, I'll show you something ain't wrong. You come see what Bill's boy brought in last night. Not no damn Keye-Oat, I can tell you."

T he friend drags the fry out of the mayonnaise again and sucks it clean. The fry sags down. He lets it fall onto a plate of untouched chicken fried steak and country potatoes.

***

"When she rose up, all phantom like and bleeding out from every orifice as if her death was as fresh as a minute ago, I think I shat myself but then it was calm. I saw her bleeding for what it was and I can tell you, it was nothing dangerous or premonitory. It was like a tribute." Steven lay back on his pillow and sighed deeply. "I can tell you now just how I found her, you'll be interested, I know. She's hidden well, but there are certain distinguishing features along the path. A knotted branch, a fern that's bent and growing up the side of a beech tree, a lot of moss hanging down one side of a boulder, and some beetles rolling dung along a well worn path in the dirt. A circle of mushrooms, a break in the trees where a ray of light shines down and there, she's just sitting there quiet."

Dennis scratches his forehead. He can hear the gunshots better from here. A myriad of companion sounds drift in through the barred window: bird calls, the whoops of hunters, the yelps of dogs grazed by bullets. Once sharper than a Fennec Fox's, Dennis ears ping only dully with each successive gunshot. He swallows back panic as Steven turns cataract-speckled eyes on him. "They're so far out in the forest, Dennis."

Dennis gulps again, rearranges the chair so he isn't facing Steven and says, "I know."

"No one ever goes that far out into the forest, Dennis."

In one version of events, he watches her soundlessly from the exaggerated afternoon shadow of a lone gas pump as she clambers up the steep sharp steps of a bus, clutching a single valise at the bottom of her stomach, thinking she is alone at last, feeling as if she is being watched. Comforted by those invisible eyes like they are the eyes of someone wise and eternal.

***

It has long been the case that those closest to the wild fear the wild the most. It's like being in a flood zone. Five miles away from the river, the inevitable flooding seems innocuous. The house is on stilts, you have flood insurance and a canoe. All of your valuables are on the second floor. The children know how to swim. You confront the terror of your world being washed in silty river water with preparedness and calm, every six or seven months, by waxing the canoe and sealing things in Ziploc bags.

When you are eleven feet from the river, you confront the inevitable possibility of flood when you wake to hear the waves lapping on the banks, when you are weeding the garden, when you are making lunch in the kitchen watching the rushing spring snow melt edge up the shore, lap over the sides of the levy, trickle onto the driveway.

Flooding seems much more of a threat when the water is visible from your bedroom window.

This is why Dennis lives in the center of town. Although wilderness surrounds him, he can't hear it lapping at the banks as well as he used to.

***

Gloria stands with a stick in her hand on the top of a pile of rocks downstream from the elementary school. Her hair is braided high on her head, her cheeks are pink and vaguely freckly. Her eyes are narrowed into a squint.

She is angry with her mother. Her mother doesn't understand her. Her mother doesn't understand anything. Her mother doesn't even understand her father. Her mother seems like not her mother. She kicks a rock into the river. It bounces on the shallow bottom and pops back up before coming to rest in a deep pool where a small fish bolts away from it, scuttling straight out into the current where it is swept up and out of sight. Gloria wants to read in her room. She wants to back the car down the driveway every day and make breakfast before school. She is smart enough to know what her mother means when she says: "Go find a young boy." She is not dumb. She will find a young boy the way other girls find young boys. She will find a young boy for her mother.

Just as she was thinking this thought, a boy wielding a stick similar to her own emerges from the tangle of blackberry bushes on the opposite bank. Her first reaction is to think, "Oh boy, it must hurt to walk through all of those prickly bushes," but this thought is immediately followed by another: "Oh, here we are."

The boy is shirtless and brown, from dirt or sun it is impossible to tell. Gloria waves to him: "Hey, hey!" but he doesn't turn to look at her. He is looking upstream, toward the soccer fields of the school on her side of the river. Another boy emerges from the bushes beside him, wearing a black mask and a cape. Soon a third boy and a fourth have joined the first

209

two, one with a horse mask, the other a plastic axe. Gloria waves again, throws a rock into the bushes, and slides down to the water's edge. "Hey!"

None of the boys turn. Gloria thinks a moment, she examines her clothes, unbuttons her blouse, and hikes her pink denim skirt all the way up to her rib cage. There we go, she thinks. "Hey!" They stare blankly in the direction of the soccer fields. Gloria can't see what they are staring at from down on the bank, but she doesn't think she can climb all the way back up. Instead she takes off her shoes and wades out into the water, which is freezing. Feet numbed, she steps out farther. The bottom of the river is soft and slippery. Her left foot slides down one rock and lands with a crack on another. A little translucent cloud of blood blossoms up into the water and is swept off by the current until only a small red thread of fluid trickles out of her heel. It doesn't hurt, so she continues on. The number of boys has grown while she was struggling across the river. There are seven now on the opposite bank. They are watching her now. One of them is laughing, but the rest look sympathetic. She scowls at them and clambers up the steep opposite bank, clutching at blackberry bushes to drag herself up.

A boy with dog ears and a fake plastic nose bends down and offers her a hand. He hoists her up through the blackberries, which drag at her clothes and the skin of her legs. It feels like a bad sunburn. Then before the dog boy has put her on her feet, they take off running in a pack. Gloria is not her PE teacher's favorite student for nothing, though, and she sprints after them.

***

He is glad when the sounds of gunshots and stomping boots do not carry into the heart of the forest. He feels waves of pressure standing in the claustrophobic silence as panic and frustration swell in his chest. He will never find it, which is distressing. No one will ever find it, which is comforting. His father-in-law has already found it, which is…impossible.

The road is slicker than usual. Dennis can feel the wheels slipping beneath him, no traction on the turns. And he keeps seeing bright yellow eyes in the foliage at the side of the road. It is unnerving. They are everywhere, like they say. Maybe those men are right to be out here shooting them. There is obviously some sort of infestation.

Ten miles from the Mackley Park turn-off, he rolls down the window and slows to a crawl. Rain is pinging off the glass and the hood, sizzling slightly as it hits the hot metal. He strains his ears to hear beyond the engine and the tinny sound of rain. A thunderous howling echoes off the sides of the mountain. Thousands of them, still. It is getting dark.

***

In one version of events, he kills her in the forest, leaving her ripe and swelling body naked in the crook of a tree, legs spread to birth into the shadowed and featureless forest an endless series of plagues and pestilences.

***

Gloria realizes she is falling behind. Her slashed heel starts to sting. Her thorn-whipped legs and arms burn, her sweaty face is beet red and puffy from panting for breath as they bolt up through hills so steep they have to climb on all fours to stay upright. She can still see Dog Ears in the distance, his bare feet kicking up sticks, moss and dirt as he hops through the trees. She is on her knees, one elbow on the ground. Her mother is probably worried; her father will be getting home soon. It seems like a good idea to turn back and it is obvious at this point that she will not be getting any action from these fellows.

Someone at the front stops and turns around. It is Horse Mask. He might be looking at her, although it is hard to tell where his eyes are pointing underneath the mask. She stands up. "I'm leaving, this isn't fun." She turns, hoping to make a dramatic exit, but she slips on the hill and skids down several yards on her back. A sound of murmuring grows louder as Dog Ears and another boy clamber after her, sliding through the leaves like snakes.

They grab her arms, one under each elbow, and hoist her up between them. At this distance, they seem much smaller than they did and she is embarrassed. She tries to pull down her skirt a little, to cover her muddy thighs but they are gripping her too tightly and she cannot get her arms free. She writhes and struggles but their small hands are vice-grips, tightening like Chinese finger traps as she struggles.

***

"Your daughter is at Amelia's for the weekend," Kim says without turning as Dennis enters the kitchen. Something unidentifiable is boiling on the stovetop, a sort of greenish paste. Dennis peers into the pot for as long as he can stand before hoisting himself up onto the counter.

"Don't sit on the counter, Dennis," his wife snaps. He slides off. There is a moment of silence then she says, "If it wasn't just down the street, I'd…" she shakes her head. Kim spends most of her life shaking her head. "I spent all day at Michael and Karen's and you won't believe what the boys have been dragging in off the mountain."

Dennis grunts, picks at the lip of the counter.

"Don't pick at that." Dennis curls his fingers into his palm. "Those animals are so thick up there you can shoot blind and kill twenty. That's what they're saying." Dennis scoffs.

His wife scowls, seems disappointed.

Dennis reaches out a hand to touch her shoulder and she whips it away, splattering the wall with green goop from the stove. "Damn it!"

His wife's face mutates once again into the black-eyed, pupil-less mask he has seen before. And he knows what is going on.

***

They are climbing up. The hill steepens under their feet. Gloria's white tennis shoes are streaked with sap and mud. Young boys float effortlessly over the wasting pine needles around her, ducking in and out of sight, a constantly shifting swarm of masked faces and torn clothing. As they climb they become more ghoulish. They become whiter as darkness drops down over the mountain. Gunshots crack in Gloria's ears. Up ahead, a glimmer of light like a hearth fire.

***

Dennis picks his way through the foot-deep pulp of decayed newspapers like a gazelle. The door, slick and wet, stands slightly ajar and he pushes it open, wondering if one of the nurses is changing the sheets, dreading the sight of pale grey slacks stretched to amazing proportions by the giant backside of an old nurse. His father-in-law is in love with one of the nurses. Dennis can never remember which one. The man has loved her from the first day. Until the madness set in, she was his one obsession. A voice murmurs in the bedroom as Dennis turns the corner and steps over the carpet sticky and stiff with dried urine and mildew. But when Dennis nudges the door open with the tip of one finger no one is in the room.

"You take her by the hand and lead her to the woods. You take her to the place you knew you all would go. You lie her down and worship her. You take her by the hand and lead her there," the voice whispers

Dennis's feet seem locked to the floor. He tries to move, to run, to look around but all he can do is stiffen more. He has lost control of all his muscles. He nearly shits himself before his weakened ears finally hone in on the source of the sound and his feet carry him, breathless, to the window. Under the sill, in the cool sand beside the apartment wall, a small boy with half a Barbie and half a bologna sandwich sits whispering to the sandwich. The Barbie is bottom-less, a pen puncture through one eye. As Dennis watches from the empty bedroom of his father-in-law, the boy stabs the Barbie with a penknife and whirls around to stare at Dennis.

He hisses like a cat through the false plastic beak of a black bird. Then he runs, leaving the sandwich and the Barbie behind.

***

"Dad?"

***

"There's a place, son, out back of these woods, far past the other side of this mountain, all that was south as south as south goes, all downhill, all clear and washed out by fire underneath the trees. In that place a flower grows that'll only bloom when it gets a breath of fire. The seeds lie dormant until the winds bring the scent of flame and then they start to grow up, up, up. The seven plagues all come from the bloated belly of one pregnant bitch, son and that bitch is the earth. The hellish blossom comes and it sweeps across the ground like its own wave of wildfire. Devouring everything that remains. Then in the night its seeds drop into the lush bed of its smothering leaves and they grow swaddled in the warm organic heat of their mother. And when they're big enough, they come for you. They come for you so hard."

***

Kim's eyes dart from fire to fire, unfocused, looking through the reflection, almost opaque with roosters crowding the furniture in the living room. Her dining room expands into the night, it stretches out parallel to the house, all the way to the mountain where sparks ignite and die, ignite and die. Her child is safe in the kitchen of another mother. Kim imagines her child in the fires, in the night in a vision so vivid and pure that it might be clairvoyance. She gasps and smiles. She chuckles to herself.

***

Dennis is speeding up the mountain in pursuit of his ancient and demented father-in-law when a blue heron swoops low in front of his windshield. The antennae of the car nicks the birds tremendous wing and it crumples mid-flight, into a diminished heap on the side of the highway. Dennis slams on his breaks and backs up. He watches in the rear-view mirror as the bird is smothered in the blackness of night. Then the night around the bird shimmers and the blue heron is covered in black birds.

***

"Where are you my good, sweet girl? Where are you? You led me to your home so many nights, so many nights I followed you while you dreamt and now where are you? My feet are old, I only have a minute and I'm so cold now. Come on and find me, lead me where you know we all must go."

***

The boys are skeletons now. Skeletons in plastic masks and overalls so grave-tattered they could be ancient sail cloth or loose thread, they shudder with rasping breath after rasping breath, into the empty body cavity, out of the muscle-less larynx, into the empty body cavity.

215

"Children…"

Gloria shivers in her pink denim skirt and modest cotton bra. Her hair has become the home of four beetles and a white moth, which has mistaken her shimmering golden strands for the winding beams of the moon. The skeleton boys throw her down before a woman who looks very familiar. The woman is breathing through her teeth and alternately gasping and moaning as if in the middle of amazing and invisible intercourse. Beside her is a backpack filled with fruit so molded and mushy that it is only distinguishable by the overpowering smell and a swarm of flies that surround it.

"Children…"

Gloria recognizes the woman. She knows the woman.

Gloria throws up suddenly. Her vomit is warm and pink. The woman is Gloria. Gloria is hugely pregnant, her mouth is wet and black. She is tied to the base of a tree with a bungee cord that has cut through the fat of her belly to the muscle beneath. The wound is festering.

Gloria's legs are spread wide and something is crowning. Gloria is staring as something red, vein-speckled and hot steams out of her.

She is screaming. The skeleton boys are rasping skeleton laughter.

The thing crowning is blacker than the night.

***

When the blackbirds clear, the heron is a collection of small, hollow bones and a single black eye more doleful and sad than any eye still socketed.

"Dad!" Dennis cries into the forest. "Dad! Steve! Steven!" He struggles to listen but the sound of repeated gunfire is almost deafening. Gunfire and howling.

***

"You have been giving birth for so long, my sweet child. You have been growing them up inside you for a thousand years. Finally, here they come." Steve rubs his graying hands together, trying to feel the creases and the knuckles again but all he feels is like a few soft mittens, formless and textureless. She is not answering. She is not calling back to him when he calls out. Only coyotes are calling back. He pauses. He thinks. Of course. Only the coyotes are calling back. He sprints into the underbrush toward the howling.

***

When her grandfather appears beside her, Gloria is alone with Gloria. She is heaving and panting again. The skeletons have all lain down around her like suckling piglets. They slowly rub their small plastic faces up and down her round hot belly.

He kneels but Gloria is too afraid to look at him and then the crowning head rips through the cervix in a shower of afterbirth. It is a blackbird and it is followed by another. And another. And another.

***

Dennis sits on the curb at the entrance to the Mackley Park trail. A man and his two sons are dragging an animal the size of a moose across the parking lot. The hide is completely stripped away already, huge chunks of meat tear off as they paint a red carpet to their jeep. They heave the creature onto the roof with a system of levers and pulleys already in place and drive off, blood and tissue careening off the back of the Jeep, taken up by the wind and scattered back into the woods where eyes and tongues examine it closely.

The carpet of blood stretches up into the forest, blanketing the path that the body has cleared in the undergrowth.

"Find yourself a man, Gloria, find yourself a nice young boy to occupy your time. Put on that short skirt and get the hell out of the house."

***

A swarm of black birds is bursting from Gloria as Steven and Gloria watch. She is stiller than stone and as cold as a corpse. Steven is kneeling, arms outstretched before the swarm when Gloria stands, silhouetted, almost naked and pale before the snowstorm of black feathers. And her father is coming through the trees quite suddenly. He is running, loping up the hill like a jackal on thin legs, his face the menacing grimace Gloria sees in her nightmares. He is clutching a kitchen knife in one hand, a rope in the other.

He says nothing as he deftly plunges the kitchen knife between the ribs of Gloria. When she falls, the scene her body obscured is visible in the half-light. Steven kneels. Gloria is black-lipped, birthing a horde of blackbirds, which speed up, out of the womb, into a tornado in the sky ripping through the forest canopy. Coyotes are scattering. All beasts are scattering in the dimness.

Dennis kneels near his daughter and cradles her head as Steven sings and cries and the blackbirds twirl past them, straight up into the sky.

RULES OF APPROPRIATE CONDUCT

At eleven years old, a child should know its way around a giraffe. That is to say, given a giraffe, a child should know which end is which, where to put the food and where it comes out. A child should have a fair grasp of giraffe handling, moderate experience riding the giraffe, should be capable of telling a giraffe the schedule for the day, and capable of sending the giraffe to work with a good hot meal in its stomach.

Without these basic skills, a child will never mature into the decent, hard-working, attractive, professional, self-motivated, buckled-down giraffe enthusiast that today's society expects of them.

What is and is not appropriate to teach your child about the giraffe? There have been many published reports and many opinions still circulate on the matter. The animal tendencies of the giraffe preclude any pussy-footing around the cold, hard facts of nature. It is a good idea to learn the child in all areas of natural giraffe development and behavior, even those from which the concerned adult may wish to shield their young, vulnerable offspring.

Which giraffe positions are best suited to the child's inevitably diminutive stature? It is difficult to say. Every situation is different and where the leaning windowposition may lend confidence to some children, others may prefer the backward spiraling chimney. Flexibility and adaptability are two key traits to be cultivated and developed in the young giraffe handler.

Remember!

Always use protective eyewear, kneepads, elbow pads and heavy, heat-resistant gloves when instructing, feeding, riding, or cleaning your giraffe and don't forget to have fun!

"Artichoke" published in *Bust Down the Door and Eat All the Chickens*
"Earl," "The Salmon Men" published in the *Magazine of Bizarro Fiction*
"Wives of Poor Men" published at *Housefire*
"Culture of Bacteria" published in *Nouns of Assemblage*
"Gloria" published in *In Heaven Everything is Fine: stories inspired by David Lynch*
"23,28" published in *Amazing Stories of the Flying Spaghetti Monster*
"The Drowned Ballet" published in *Innsmouth Magazine*
"Paper Nautilus" published at *New Dead Families*

OFFICIAL

CCM

GET OUT OF JAIL
* VOUCHER *

- -

Tear this out.

Skip that social event.

It's okay.

You don't have to go if you don't want to. Pick up
the book you just bought. Open to the first page.
You'll thank us by the third paragraph.

If friends ask why you were a no-show, show them
this voucher.
You'll be fine.

- -

We're coping.

CPSIA information can be obtained at www.ICGtesting.com
Printed in the USA
LVOW10s0141021215

464979LV00004B/159/P

9 781937 865528